W9-CLQ-327

BOOKS BY THOMAS MCGUANE

*The Sporting Club*
*The Bushwhacked Piano*
*Ninety-Two in the Shade*
*Panama*
*An Outside Chance*
*Nobody's Angel*
*Something to Be Desired*

# SOMETHING
# TO BE DESIRED

# Thomas McGuane

# SOMETHING TO BE DESIRED

 Random House  New York

Copyright © 1984 by Thomas McGuane

All rights reserved under International and Pan-American Copyright
Conventions. Published in the United States by Random House, Inc.,
New York, and simultaneously in Canada by Random House of
Canada Limited, Toronto.

A portion of this work previously appeared in *Vanity Fair*.

Library of Congress Cataloging in Publication Data

McGuane, Thomas.
Something to be desired.

I. Title.
PS3563.A3114S6   1984      813'.54      83–43198
ISBN 0–394–52873–5

*Manufactured in the United States of America*

9 8 7 6 5 4 3 2

FIRST EDITION

*For Count Guy de la Valdene*

There is no question that the dog
who is really ready for a big trial
is on the threshold of committing
grave mistakes.

—CHARLES MORGAN,
*On Retrievers*

# SOMETHING TO BE DESIRED

The moon lofted off the horizon to drift low over the prairie, white and imperious as a commodore. While the two walked, their shadows **1** darted over the ground and through the sage. The boy went along, concentrating on the footing, which was secure and reliable except where the washes had undercut ledges that sloughed quickly beneath them. His father strode ahead in silence, his boots making a steady beat unmodified by the boy's breathlessness. The boy still wore his baseball jersey and had a green sweater tied around his waist. The wind came out of the draws and breathed through them toward the lights of town.

"You out of breath?"

"No, sir."

"Keep moving." His father made forward in vengeance, then asked, "Do you feel like you've been stolen?"

"No, sir."

His father had returned after hiding from his mother, hiding in, of all places, Arequipa, Peru, where he had cooked on sheep dung and drunk too much and mailed deranged letters to his son until his son flunked his courses and got kicked off the baseball team. Then on a morning when the boy spent still another Saturday at home, away from his beloved third base, the father walked in and said, "What'll it be, Lucien? Where do we go?"

Lucien, a small-town boy buried in Ernest Thompson Seton, said, "Up in the hills." He was baffled by his father's dramatics but, more than anything, happy to see him again.

Now they were lost. They had been lost for two days. Not seriously lost, because they could see the lights of Deadrock; but they had lost their own camp on the rocky escarpment of the Crazy Mountains. And though they could have walked to the highway in a few hours, they still hadn't had food in days. Their feet were blistered; twice the father had curled up on the ground before walking the great circle again with fury and self-pity. When he heard the boy's hard breathing, he said, "You're a baseball player and I'm fifty. Keep walking." Lucien was silent. He thought of his books and wondered if they were still on the study-hall desk, in the nearly empty room with its clock, superintended by a history teacher one week, an English teacher another, some bored man with a paperback spending his time miserably. Lucien's sudden fall to flunking seemed strangely permanent. One upperclassman called him a forceps baby. The light of detention fell through institutional windows upon Lucien and the books that had suddenly gone dead on him. He was homesick and there was no home, nothing to fill a caissonned heart, until the blazing satisfaction of his father's arrival, descended from the inexplicable Arequipa, Peru, where Lucien pictured Indians and colonials circling his father through the divorce. It was the year of the vicuña scandal in Eisenhower's administration. The profanity of his father's departure seemed to the boy to infect national politics. Furthermore, his mother didn't want to give the family another try. "It's quits," she said of the marriage.

Lucien began to think, If we cannot find the camp, we'll have to go to Peru. Moreover, his last history lesson, possibly still open on the study-hall desk, concerned the Teapot Dome scandal. Lucien knew that Teapot Dome was out here somewhere, maybe between here and camp; and around it were the ghosts of crooks in vests and homburgs, crooks with money. He had already learned that in America the very good and the very bad had money to burn.

"If you want to give up," said his father, "we can start toward the highway." His face was charged with suffering and there was a slight whistle in his breath.

Lucien looked him over. "I don't want to quit," said Lucien. "I want to find our camp."

"We did this sort of thing at fifteen thousand feet," said his father shakily. "In the Andes." Lucien knew his father's companion in Peru, a Billings car dealer named Art Clancy, also on the run from divorce. Art weighed two hundred thirty pounds. Lucien had a harder time picturing him at fifteen thousand feet than he had picturing his father. Art was a famous lady-killer, even at his weight; he had a secret apartment and a Corvette. There was some connection between these things and the separation of Lucien's parents. One hung-over morning, according to Lucien's mother, Art Clancy and his father had joined the winter segment of a thing called the World Adventure Series. It was a tour that went to Peru, where the Indians wore stocking caps with earflaps and where Lucien's father, deprived of his secretary, wrote

5

Lucien the only handwritten letters Lucien had ever seen of his. The writing was strong and linear and spoke of romantic escape: sometimes Lucien's father was alone the romantic escapist; sometimes Lucien and his father were depicted in the letters as escaping; sometimes there was anger and glory, sometimes just anger. In all cases it was the world that was against them, a world that no longer cared for the individual with his dread of homogeneity. Sometimes not one word of the letters could be read. It was like the night Lucien's mother had made a tape recording of his father, and he went after her. Because of that, Lucien's father went out the door with the police, and the next thing was the World Adventure Series to Peru with Art Clancy. Lucien's mother called Lucien's father a coward, a strong word.

Lucien began to know where they were. He could have said so right away. Instead, he took a very slight lead until they were around the bottom of the low cliff. His father didn't know they were on the trail again. Above them, the rock was black and spilled stars in a bright path to the lighted clouds. It was the perfect trail to get jumped on from above, by a cougar or a gook: Lucien had no idea who lived around here. But he did know it was more than a backdrop for his father and himself, more than an illustrated letter. For some reason he didn't tell his father they were on the trail once more. He could hear the whistle in his father's breath as though some small rigid thing were stuck in his throat, some forceful thing.

A cloud of crows lifted from a depression between small hills, revealing the most remarkable hot spring imaginable, a deeply colored blue hole with pale steam blowing from its surface to tangle its streamers in the trunks of sage. For a brief time the two forgot their

6

troubles as they floated in thermal blue. They saw the world through a gentle fog and they talked in the simplest statements.

Lucien's father spotted some ranch buildings in the distance. "This must be private," he said; and they left.

Then you could see their camp, a grim, improperly erected pup tent with canned food in a pile by its entrance. They had been gone nearly two days, and when his father saw the tent, he groaned and trotted toward it. He threw himself on the ground beside the cans; his curved and exhausted back heaved for a long time. Lucien wondered whether this was a heart attack. "Are you okay?" he asked but got no answer. He hated himself for not knowing appropriate first aid.

His father slung himself up. He said, "We better eat. We better eat now."

Lucien began to build a fire. There was plenty of dry wood. There were matches and a patented product that he squirted into the wood. In a moment they had fire and heat.

"Our time in the desert is at an end," said Lucien's father. Lucien had not thought of it as desert. He thought the two days following the sun around a long corner had been beautiful. He wasn't sure in what way his father had been present, but his father had been present in the minimum way a boy will accept.

The tent was an old one, bought by mail when Lucien was in the first grade, for a trip to the Boundary Waters of Minnesota, a trip they were unable to make because of the recession, or something about middle management. The tent had been treated to waterproof it, a tar smell. The moon outside revealed the weave of the cloth. Lucien watched his father's wonderfully peaceful sleep. He couldn't make out if he was in worse trouble at school and would never be returned to the baseball team; or if his father's terrific intervention canceled that world and its rules. In fact, he couldn't exactly make out if his father was glad to be back. It was as if the same master stood over them with a stick and not only drove them but drove them in circles, around the mountains, around their camp, around their tin cans.

His father had brought a fancy Zenith radio for the trip, so that they would not be surprised by weather. Lucien got nine countries on it. He turned it as low as he could and dialed away at his sleeplessness. He got Mexico, an exciting thing in 1958. The speaker from Mexico spoke very rapidly, reminding Lucien that he was flunking Spanish. If he picked up *muy* once, he picked it up a hundred times. Then he ran the six-foot antenna out the tent flap and dialed some more: he got an English-language Baptist station right in the middle of Port-au-Prince, Haiti, right where they have voodoo, talking about Our Lord Jesus Christ; not at all the way a radio Baptist would carry on stateside. You could tell the people of Haiti had put a civil tongue in his head. Then Lucien got rough northern voices he could not understand. Maybe they belonged to Russians.

He turned back to Haiti. Cold wind stirred the tent sides, a rocky wind that murmured through the imprecations of the stranded preacher in Haiti so anxious to make friends among the heathen that he pronounced their country "I.T.," as the Haitians did; the wind murmured over the tired Peruvian traveler and a son still early in his journey.

The day broke blue and northern on the basin of gravel, a basin lined with thin glittering springs and the delicacies of vegetation that spilled their edges all the way to the brisk willows at the creek bottom. The creek turned south till it fell off the end. Someone's lost saddle horse stood exactly where the creek fell into pure blue sky, alternately grazing and staring across the gravelly basin to their camp. Lucien's first thought was to catch him, ride him back to school and get to play third base again.

I could never catch him, he thought. He remade the fire for breakfast, building it in a single blast with the patented fire-starter, a flame as tall as Lucien that wavered ominously toward the tent, then shrank into the firewood peaceably. His father woke to the smell of hash and eggs, and crawled forth with a bleak squint into broad daylight.

"You left the radio on, Lucien. The battery is dead." His father doubled over to scrutinize a blister on his heel, displacing its liquid between opposing thumbs. "God-almighty," he said.

They breakfasted and Lucien cleaned the aluminum plates in the spring. The cold water congealed the grease to the metal, and he had to scour them with sand to make them clean. Lucien was conscious of his father staring at the peaks, plain rock jumping out of ground that looked as soft as a stream bank. "No wonder nobody lives here, no wonder they stay back in town," his father said. "There's no reason to be here. You come here to get something and then out you go. Look at that poor damn horse. Can you feature that?"

This gave Lucien no feeling whatsoever, not unless that in itself was a feeling. It was like hitting a baseball and having it just not come down. You could hardly call it a fielding error.

His father circled the tent slowly, digging a finger into

9

his disordered hair, inventorying the camp, the camp that a few days ago had been erected as a gateway to an improved world.

"We're looking at under a hundred bucks," said his father, standing at their camp. "Let's walk away from it." Lucien listened, awaiting some further information, but that was all: leave it.

They had nothing to carry, nor the struggle of climbing; Lucien's father led the way with a jaunty step. Part of the mission was completed. The lights of Deadrock were reduced to the dimensional outlines of the little burg; and there were brief gusts of stink from the hot springs south of town. Lucien wondered why unpleasantness and healing were always connected.

"I'm afraid I feel a little guilty," said Lucien's father with a laugh. "A little guilty, a little hungry and a little thirsty."

"Guilty for what?"

"Taking you away from school."

Lucien walked on for a minute, scuffing along the dry, stony trail. "I wasn't doing well," he said. "You didn't do any harm."

"I'm sure I did a *lot* of harm," said his father. Lucien wondered why he always made his father feel so guilty. They had had so very few adventures together, but each one of them made his father burn with guilt. Maybe they shouldn't try to have adventures; the thought choked Lucien with sadness, but maybe it was true. Not if the adventures were just going to make his father burn with guilt. They had gone to Cabo San Lucas, and his father burned like a martyr because it was the first trip they had made that reflected the deterioration of Lucien's parents' marriage. That trip at least had been on a school vacation, so the sense of irresponsibility had not been so hard on his father as this time. Lucien knew that this time his father felt more like a kidnapper than an adventurer.

For the last half mile the trail was only a ledge in the granite. Beyond the ledge, soaring birds were seen from above, now and then diving feetfirst into the prairie. Their car could be discerned too: an almost vertical view, a rectangle of paint, like the toy car Lucien used to scuff one-handed on the carpet at home. That was back when his mother and father had had famous parties where they displayed their outstanding dancing and where Lucien, already dying to please, had trained himself to be a perfect bartender, silent and friendly, willing to overrule the jigger for family friends, later listening through the floor for the bellowed jokes and the Valkyrian laughs of the wives. It was when the census bureau harried Lucien's father for declaring himself an entrepreneur; Lucien still wasn't sure what that was, but all the adults banded together to throw parties to fight the census bureau, to pass the hat, to declare their faith in entrepreneurs, a category that the census bureau would not accept. It was exciting. Lucien was the pubescent speedy bartender, who bracketed new people in town, the probational ones, with his strict jigger. Then suddenly things got so exciting that his father tore off to Peru with the man who sold him his last car: a car different from the plain business model the trail wound toward; the car Art Clancy sold his father was a Thunderbird, and now his mother had it. She had the house and she had the assets. Plus she had done something Lucien couldn't quite fathom—she had let the memberships go. And now they

were gone, his father had said dolorously: the memberships are gone.

They drove toward Deadrock, where they had rented the
car. They weren't going to turn the rental in today; his
father promised over and over that they wouldn't turn it
in today, as though Lucien cared. "We've had this car for
nearly half a week," his father crowed, "and it's got less
than fifty miles on it!" As they drove, Lucien listened to
stories of the living descendants of the Incas, how they
hid gold in lakes, cut out hearts, sacrificed virgins. He
heard of the astonishment of these small people, with
their great Andean chests and earflaps, at the sight of
Art Clancy's Corvette. Peru had been quite a deal. The
Indians tried to put their hands all over the car. Art
Clancy spoke to them in a kind of imitation Khrushchev.
"Hands off," he told the little Incas. "Gives a shot in the
head." The year of Cabo San Lucas there had been a long
aftermath of Mexican. "Eees good!" stood for approval.
When Lucien hooked a trout in the ditch back of the
house, his mother cried out, "Feesh! Eees good!"
    Lucien suspected that his mother was as much on his
father's mind as she was on his own. It was his father's
quietness as he made his way across the river bridge, then
the railroad tracks. Maybe Lucien's mother should have
thrown his father out; but when she did, she threw everything out and maybe she shouldn't have done that. Who
would ever know? Nobody. It infected everything from
daybreak to baseball. It infected all things. It was a
pestilence.

They drove into Deadrock. They were traveling light.
The town crouched in front of the terrific mountains to

the south, great wildly irregular peaks that seemed to say to the little town, Don't try anything. No one strolled the streets as Lucien and his father sat in the parked rental car. There were plenty of people visible but they just emerged from one store or bar and darted into another, short sudden arcs, escaping the same general gaze. This irresolute air suited Lucien and his father perfectly. The day felt too early and too late. Before the divorce, this had been his father's hometown too.

"We better get a room," his father said.

He restarted the car and began to hunt for a place. There were a couple of satisfactory hotels which they cruised past at very low speed. His father looked at them critically, then leaned out into the warm air to crane up at their higher stories either to evaluate their height and substance or to hope for an anomalous penthouse, more satisfactory than the lower rooms, rooms to which Lucien was sure his father referred when he uttered the single word "dandruff."

Then impatiently he gunned out onto Parkway and found Deadrock's only motel, a new place. In 1958 a motel was a pretty exciting thing, comfort and life alongside your car. Now Lucien saw that his father was okay once again, that there was volition and not a mind wandering through things spoilt. And the reproachful presence of your own child. Yes, Lucien felt that now.

Lucien's father went inside to get them a room. He came out with a ballpoint, wrote down the license number and went back inside. Then he came back and jumped in the car heartily. "Fifteen B, I love it! 'B'! They only have one floor! You ought to see the owner. Get the feeling you don't take a room and the bank pounces on him." His father smiled wide with charity. Lucien

13

glanced over and saw the motel lady, drawing back the venetian blinds, caught. He waved a little.

The room was another world: up-to-date, lightless. There were little things on the bedspread you could pick at. Lucien's father made his way sideways to each reproduction on the wall, thrummed his fingers on top of the TV, counted out ten dollars and weighted them with an ashtray. "I'm going out for a belt. I'm late and you get hungry, here's ten bucks." He was gone in a shudder of daylight.

Lucien read the welcome to Big Sky and thumbed the motel Bible. Kukla, Fran and Ollie wouldn't be on television for a while. He pulled the curtain and saw their car was gone: he'd never heard it start up. He wondered if anyone would get some use out of their tent; maybe the owner of that horse—it would make a good combination for a man wanting to travel out in all those hills and mountains. He lay down for a moment trying to get control of himself. Very soon he wasn't moving.

He woke up in the middle of the night. His father was standing bolt upright in his shorts, arm outstretched, finger pointing, a dynamo of rejection, a god casting someone out. "Go!" he roared.

Indeed, someone was being cast out; but she felt very strongly that she had not been given time to dress. She complained with acid bitterness as she crawled through her own clothing, holding individual articles up toward the bathroom light for rough identification.

"*Go!*" roared his father.

"I'm *gone*," she whined. "But not like this."

She struggled a bit more, stood and slanted through the small opening Lucien's father made for her into the night.

Lucien listened to his father walking around, stopping only for long sighs. Finally:

"Lucien?"

"I'm awake."

"I'm sorry . . . ?"

"I'm awake, sir."

"How long have you been awake?"

"Not long," Lucien said.

"Lucien, when you were a small boy, I let you have lots of pets, hamsters, rabbits and so on. Do you remember I allowed that?"

"Yes, sir, I do."

"That was so you could learn about animals, about how we are all animals."

"Yes, sir."

"And now I want to call Momma."

He got the night operator or the morning operator, whichever, and revealed to Lucien's mother that they were no longer out in the mountains. "Momma," he said. "I'm with Lucien. We want to come home to you, Momma." Lucien could not devise an attitude toward this. His father suddenly fell to listening. He repeated "uh huh" a number of times in a deeper and flatter voice. He waved Lucien into the bathroom, then waved the door shut behind him. Lucien leaned on the faucet, turning it microscopically until a drop of water came out, shut it off, and did it again. Then he heard his father call for him.

When he went into the bedroom the reading lamp was on and his father sat right next to it, weeping, silently with heaving shoulders.

"What's the matter, Pop, can't we go home?" Lucien was scared.

"It's not that—" He sobbed for a few more minutes

and composed himself carefully. "Art Clancy was shot and killed by his girlfriend," he sobbed. "In Arequipa, Peru."

Lucien's father had coached him carefully as they walked across town from the motel. They stood in front of their house while his father ran a finger around the inside of his collar, then gave Lucien a quick, conspiratorial nod. He knocked. In a moment the door opened and there was his mother, all dressed up.

"When's lunch!" Lucien and his father cried together.

She looked from one to the other. "That hungry gang of mine," she said with a warm smile and turned into the house for her men to follow.

Chili was gone. He knew very well that his mother might have disposed of the small, blue, merry bird; or at least given the bird away, purely on the basic of its Hispanic name. Lucien was sure she pictured Clancy of Peru in his shantung suits, his Corvette and his bad Spanish in a way that made a parakeet named Chili look bad. He already suspected that her greeting was camouflage, so the crack of his mother's hand against his father's face came as not much of a surprise. His father just took it. There was little else he could do. Raising his hands in self-defense would have made him a pantywaist in the eyes of his own son.

"I'll go," said Lucien's father.

"Where? Peru?" Her long patrician face always looked surprised when she was angry. What many took for astonishment was in fact a prelude to hysterical fury. "You and your Peru!"

Then Lucien's father did something very strange and

16

yet wholly characteristic of him: he waved to an imaginary person in the window behind her; when she turned to look, he flattened her with a tremendous blow.

His father left the room, straight through the French doors into the side yard, where the dog hid in its Tudor house, the chain making an abrupt circuit back into the little doorway as it always did in a family dispute. He sauntered over the high ground beside the lilacs and took a final glance into the living room before retiring to the guest room over the garage.

Lucien's mother still lay on the floor, lightly fingering the discoloration around her left eye. "I'm a chump if I don't call a cop," she said, using a diction she seldom used unless she was trying to reveal the actual sordid texture she saw in her life. If this had all happened to an acquaintance, she would have said, "She's deluded if she doesn't call a policeman." She slung herself upright, got to her feet and headed for the stairs. "You had better find something to eat, Lucien. I'm in no shape to help you men. Not today. Perhaps not ever." Lucien felt the excitement return at these last words. He still felt the raw electricity in the air. He made a sandwich.

When he had finished it, he went over to the guest room. His father was sitting on the edge of the bed like a man on his first night at boot camp. "I couldn't let her go on like that, kiddo," he said. "Not with you there." He looked up to see if Lucien was buying it. Lucien let no expression cross his face. "I don't even know whose side you're on." He flung himself on the bed with his hands behind his head, staring at the ceiling. "Out in those wide open spaces . . . now, that was another thing entirely. Out where they don't hamstring a man for standing a little tall."

Lucien took a pitcher of ice water up to his mother. She drank hungrily, as though she had come in from a long journey only moments before. "I wonder who the real ringleader on that Peru trip was. Now Clancy is dead. I guess I'll never know, will I? Clancy would have told me because Clancy knew better than to cross swords with me. Do you follow, Lucien? Of course you don't, you little angel with silver wings, you. . . . Brandy."

Lucien went downstairs and brought back the brandy and a snifter. His mother had a candle going in her room by now and swirled and heated her glass as she sipped. "No, Lucien, between your father and Art Clancy there wasn't a stick of decency." She held her glass so the candle danced on the other side of it. She squinted and continued. "Clancy? I hope he fries in hell." Lucien shuddered at this, to him, wholly realistic idea. "Your father is not man enough to deserve such spectacular punishment." She spat. "Did you have a lovely time out in the country?"

"Yes, Mom."

"What did you see?"

"Just this horse."

"Doesn't sound like much of a trip."

"It's hard to describe."

"Well," she said, "at least you're not old enough to have gotten into any trouble. Though that too, I suppose, is just around the corner."

His mother's search for the combination that would tie them in an awful knot had begun to strike Lucien right in the stomach. His mother fished a mirror out of her purse and sized up the swelling on her face. Then she patted it with a powder puff, as though she wished it could not be seen. She drew out a picture and held it close to her face. "Clancy," she said. "Who would have ever thought?"

There was something in the air that Lucien didn't like, didn't like at all. After this kind of talk, no one in the family would know to turn up the heat in the winter or close the windows when it rained or put antifreeze in the Thunderbird in November. No one would remember to send crazy Aunt Marie a thank-you note when she forgot to send a Christmas present, and Aunt Marie's Christmas would be ruined.

The long night got longer. First Lucien's father stole down for a late snack and nearly collided with his mother. Lucien watched from the couch. The French bread under his arm, the six-pack of imported beer, the cheese and the fruit all fell to the floor. "It takes quite a bit to spoil your appetite, doesn't it, Gene?"

"Hunger and grief are absolutely compatible, you goddamned whore," replied his father. "Lucien," he added, "get your mother a sweater. It's cold down here."

Lucien ran his hand up the long, cool banister and watched the candlelight from his mother's room flicker on the carpet. First he got the sweater, the cableknit cardigan she wore when sick, then he rifled the purse for Clancy's picture. He cut that up with his jackknife and flushed it down the toilet. He read a quick couple of pages from the Kinsey Report lying by the bed, and went downstairs, where he found his parents hugging and cooing. Tex Benecke's band was playing "Maria Elena" on the record player, a sure sign of new weather. "I love you, you bugger," said his father, "you know I do." This last was slightly crooned to the big-band sound in the air.

Lucien went out and sat in the rock garden and

thought about the hills and the tent they had left and the old rock sheepherder's monument that looked out over the valley of Bangtail Creek. He thought of the rental car, the freedom vehicle that had almost succeeded, and his father banishing devils in the motel. The laughter and toasts that came from the house now seemed like a home team faithfully cheered for a bad loss. His father's occasional riggish chuckle made Lucien uncomfortable.

The next thing he knew, Father Moore's big car came pouring up the driveway. The minister, not knowing he was observed by Lucien, climbed angrily out of the car, knocked and went in. Father Moore always bought season tickets with Lucien's father. In years past they had gotten into lots of trouble together. By the time Lucien went inside, Father Moore, in his sweatshirt and khakis, had a big drink of his own and was joining in on the spirit of things. Lucien's mother hung slightly forward from the waist in her cableknit cardigan and did not quite seem to know what was going on. The stars that had illuminated the rock garden were invisible through the brightly lit living-room windows.

Lucien's parents stood shoulder to shoulder. His father was hugely animated and shouted everything he said. Lucien was given a small pillow for the ring. Father Moore—"Dicky" Moore—had his limp Bible splashed open on one hand while the other held his drink. He rattled through the marriage ceremony, stopping once for a refill; and at the end, when Lucien's mother was to say "I do," she instead screamed, "The man I love died in Peru!" and threw herself to the floor.

Lucien's father went out the door, never to return. Lucien sat once more on the starry lawn listening to

Father "Dicky" Moore move through the vegetation, nervously murmuring his name.

When Lucien was an adult, when rain whirled up through the hayfield and scattered birds with its force, he heard his own name in the rock garden and knew he was free, as the saying once went, to dispose himself as he pleased.

•–•–•–•–•–•–•–•–•–•–•–•–•–•–•–•–•–•–•–•–•–•–•–•–•–•–•–•–•–•–•–•–•–•–•–•–•–•–•–•–•

For almost five years Lucien and his mother **2** lived alone on the street behind the library. They lived on alimony, child support and donations of relatives. Lucien seldom saw his father and seldom heard from him, except very occasionally in the form of highly emotional letters on hotel stationery.

Next door there lived a family with two sons; the father was an executive with Montana Power, but mainly they were displaced southerners. The father had gone to the Virginia Military Institute, and the only books he owned were the series *Lee's Lieutenants*. This man, when drinking, encouraged his boys in a violent world, which resulted in Lucien's receiving many a thrashing at their hands. They helped Lucien learn to think of himself as, first of all, a man of considerable sensitivity, and a ladies' man, not like the two next door who fought, masturbated and picked their noses. Still, Lucien impressed hardly anyone in those days gone by. His mother, a day-long tippler, always called him a "prize boob" around seven in the evening.

Lucien began to run in the hills, not like a genuinely

solitary boy but like one with a highly charged view of his own importance. He had a paper route and with the proceeds bought a horse and paid for its pasture out in the Crazies. He always took his sketch pad with him and drew what he thought he was seeing. His heroes were Ernest Thompson Seton and Theodore Roosevelt. Like all boys, he dreamed of consequentiality, and of romantic unrest. In school he was a poor student who tested in the high percentiles that set educators gambling: he was recommended to the college of his choice. Later, when he went out the door to school, his mother followed him and didn't stop until she got to Florida, from which state she occasionally called around nine o'clock Eastern Standard Time to address Lucien as a "prize boob." Lucien then used concepts larger than he could handle, and accused her of being a Jezebel. Being called a Jezebel triggered some new change in Lucien's mother; and with that, she began to tell Lucien that she was disappointed in him. It seemed a bigger change. From then on, this disappointment would be her principal theme. "You are the leading killjoy of my life," she assured him. "God will pay you back for disappointing me."

Lucien worked his way through the state university as a pizza chef, setting log chokers, as a tool-pusher and, home in the summers, as a cowboy, a fencer and an irrigator. He was a valuable ranch hand and a superb horseman.

In his first year of college he dated two girls from his hometown, Emily and Suzanne. Under Emily he was going to be a rancher and a painter of sporting subjects on the order of Thomas Eakins. Under Suzanne he would grasp desperately at his deep testability, land himself among the upper percentiles and, having trained himself only generally, go off to Latin America for the United States Information Agency, spraying leaflets on the mestizo millions. He married Suzanne.

Emily loved a medical student the entire time she saw Lucien. Later that student became a doctor, and later she married him. Emily was a raving beauty with electrifying black eyes, and she had been seeing the doctor-to-be since she was in high school. Though they had passed each other in the high school's corridors a thousand times, Emily had no idea who Lucien was. By way of compensation, she slept with him on their first meeting at college. Lucien fell so immediately in love, he hoped she was pregnant. She used to ask him where he had been all her life in such a vague way, he knew she didn't mean it. He cooked her soufflés on the nights the doctor-to-be was studying, and she made love to him between classes or read to him from the hippie books that were just then hitting the ag schools. She made him make love to her when she talked to her parents on the phone. Lucien thought it was some kind of psychological experiment; in fact, she often referred to Lucien as a "volunteer." Then one time the doctor-to-be nearly caught them together; Lucien hid in the closet, and Emily took great pains to seduce the doctor, who commented genially on her excited state. She positioned him clearly in view of the parted closet door and drove the swart medical candidate into a frenzy. When he left, Lucien made frantic love to her and Emily clawed great evil stripes in his back. He pretended to be pleased with these passionate badges; but he was barely able to put his shirt on. In blank confusion, he went into the kitchen to attempt a new soufflé. "What if he'd known I was here?" asked Lucien, thinking of the kind of violent treatment he might have received, the very kind Lee's lieutenants would have dished out.

"He knew you were here," said Emily. "He's always known you were here."

If Suzanne hadn't been beautiful that year, she might very well have been mousy. Lucien seized upon her, in his battered state at the departure of Emily, for her prettiness. Suzanne was a brown-haired, brown-eyed beauty, one who had never traded on her looks but a girl in the last of the times when looks alone would do. This left her with the curiously easygoing nature of a twenty-year-old hectored by suitors. Lucien in those years was a combination of seersucker and tragedy, though an odd kind of tragedy: certainly at first glance not a real one, not the precipitous loss that draws every heart wheeling down, but rather one that grew in effect by never quite going away.

One sixties autumn, Suzanne's genial survey of men ended. First to go was the Olympic gymnast, then the young ranch aristocrat majoring in classics at an eastern school. Right after that one the handsome orphan was dismissed, and finally the German racer. Left standing was Lucien, the curiously distracted, bookish sport who wouldn't shut up about his old squeeze. "She *left* me," Lucien wailed without shame. "Gone with a doctor who has hair on the back of his hands." The beautiful Suzanne seduced him without complaint, courted him, cooked wonderful meals which he ate absently; and made his staring, vacant presence the envy of all who saw him with this peerless girl on his arm. "You're very far away," she said. "Aren't you, Lucien?"

"Yup."

In years to come, Lucien's career, time and childbirth would tighten their grip on Suzanne's life. She became tough and smart, and she stayed beautiful. Lucien remained distracted, effective mostly in bursts of irritation. He made dreadful paintings. Later it would not surprise her when he left. But he went on explaining by phone and by mail. He fell apart. Not unkindly, she began to refer to him as a plastered saint. For Suzanne, as for all those who start out on sound principles, life went on.

Suzanne never came to Lucien's attention as deeply as Emily did. She was just as pretty but in a sunnier way. She took the position that this was a decent world for an honest player. And whenever she used her favorite remark, "It all comes out in the wash," Lucien grew defensive, taking it as a reference to Emily.

Lucien and Suzanne were married on her father's ranch on a big bend in the Shields River. Lucien's work took him immediately to Surinam, where, napping in the afternoon on their comfortable veranda, Suzanne was bitten by a bat. Since it was unusual to be bitten in the daytime, she was subjected to a painful series of rabies shots into the lining of her stomach. She played even this down, really to keep Lucien from worrying: she was pregnant with James.

Five air-conditioned years went by in the backwater posts of Central America. One sweltering September, the three of them went on holiday to Nevis, where they lived for a week in the remodeled ruins of a slave-breeding farm. It was an extraordinary week for many reasons. They had both just learned that Emily had committed a crime so awful that neither Lucien nor Suzanne spoke of it. Anyway, Emily was the past.

In the evenings they listened to the reggae bands, consorted with the gracious local people and taught James to eat conch chowder and dig for slave beads in the beach. Lucien loved his little boy very much, but with the distraction that informed all his own young life. He took him walking the ruined English fortifications and down the dock at Charlestown, where the native shipwrights caulked the long-boomed sailing lighters with ringing hammers. One afternoon they sent James walking the beach with a Nevis girl hired for the day, a girl so black and literate and merry that she supplied Suzanne with another spell of blind optimism. Lucien and Suzanne examined the ancient barrel-roofed library, the stone municipal buildings. At length they found themselves in the small chapel that felt so ancient and English that the whole anomaly of the colonial adventure rang in the tropical afternoon. Lucien stood on the flagstone grave markers of the old planters and viewed the altar where Admiral Horatio Nelson had been married. Staring at Nelson's disappearing signature in his rumpled seersucker, Lucien was suddenly poleaxed by what he saw as the lack of high romance in his life. It was one of the lowest and most paltry hours he would ever spend; and it nearly ruined him.

Their cottage was a stone building that the slaves had built. The sun had tired James, and he slept in an adjoining room. Each wall had a tall mullioned window that looked out over the rolling hills of Nevis and, well beyond, to the blue sea. There was a mosquito canopy for the bed, drawn out of the way, and treated coils of punk to be burned in the summer months. A bookcase contained a peculiar assortment of left-behind novels in various languages. It was a beautiful old room, and

Suzanne already knew that something was wrong. Lucien wanted to put it all off; but the fact that James was sleeping constrained him to say something now. He told Suzanne he wasn't going back to work. It made absolutely no sense for him to make any such statement, but he could not seem to do otherwise. Suzanne sat down with her hands in her lap. She was very tall, and that somehow made her isolation more clear. She was across the room and so very tall in the wooden chair.

"Why aren't you going back to work?"

He answered her honestly. He said, "I don't know."

"Oh. Huh," she said. "You can't even try?"

"I've gone through that. I want to start over. It's just about that simple. I'm not doing anybody any good. I'm going to be alone for a while. Does that make any sense?"

"No."

"It must, Suzanne. It must make some."

"It doesn't, because you're going back to see that cunt."

"That's not what she is."

"You're right. She's something worse than that. I just can't find the words."

"Please, Suzanne."

"I just thought the whores around the embassy would have gotten this out of your system by now." She said this in a small voice.

"Suzanne."

"I never complained about that."

"I know."

She sat quietly for a moment, looking pale. "It wasn't easy for me to not complain. You see, I'm not an up-to-date girl. Your whores got on my nerves. But I saw it as a form of insurance. Evidently it was not sufficient insurance. Because you're on the track of the queen of them all, aren't you? A lot of good it did me. I suppose I should have fucked myself a wide swath, but my heart wasn't in it, despite the fact that you don't have a single friend who didn't try. I guess that should make me feel stupid, but somehow it doesn't. It fills me with awe to see you throw away everything you have that's any good."

"You've been storing this up, darling."

"Will you be going straight back to Montana?"

All Lucien had for this was a long, feckless sigh, like an addict asked why he was killing himself with drugs. When Suzanne started crying, he stared at her as if across a state line. She shook and shook as she cried, sitting straight up in the wooden chair; she didn't make a sound. She doesn't want to wake up James, Lucien thought; but why can't I stop myself? I have the soul of a lab rat.

Lucien was alone for one day on the slave-breeding farm. He was in a kind of shock, but he hoped that shock would be one merely of transition rather than injury. If I'm so bad, he thought, they are better off without me and I have done them a good turn. With that, his spirits began to rise minutely. Sexually speaking, he thought, haven't I been a real success? I've spent thousands of hours with my ass flying and sweat spraying off me. In almost every case my partner pumped and sprayed with comparable ardor, sometimes when paid to do so. I've been the real article. He looked around himself with fear, confusion and dismay: God almighty!

That day too, he sat on the toilet daydreaming of Emily, when his half-erect penis aligned itself between the porcelain rim and the seat, and fired urine halfway across the room before he could clamp off his sphincter.

It's a monster, he thought, I know that much. Poor Old
Dick, he called it. Me and Poor Old Dick are going home.
Lucien was running absolutely blind. He had wanted to
be in the country he loved once more. He wanted to
paint, though he set only a modest store by that; he just
wanted to get a few things down, like the Indians who
traced the red ocher elk on the walls of the old hobo
caves outside of town. He felt that his life had transformed him into a functionary. He felt lost, and he knew
with absolute sincerity that Emily was certainly no cunt.

While he waited for his plane, he read the only thing
he could find, a back number of a gardeners' magazine,
an October issue. Inside, and perhaps it was his mood, he
discovered that nothing is more autumnal than a bad
writer discussing apples. And too, there was something
about wild geese mating for life that made him wish to
return to waterfowling and shoot till his barrels were hot.

Things started to become more final to him as the
plane flew north. There was nothing beneath it but
ocean, and in a short while the sun went down. When
you are drafted in wartime, he thought, it must feel like
this. You are called and you will serve. No, that wasn't
quite it. The point was, he longed to feel the fatality of
his action. When he had given his boy a hug, it was clear
that with little more emphasis the child would fall
straight into the middle of this. So their departure was
without emphasis, staged as a clear fork in the road. They
would be moved by forces to differing sections of the grid.

In any event, the process of stain had begun; he would
not have known what to call it as it sank deeper inside
him, nor been able to assess the turbulence and damage
that was to come; but it was certainly shame.

Later he would think it was early in the morning. He was going back some, but it would have had to have been before breakfast. He remembered he could smell someone cleaning a cat box at the hired man's, and there was an empty barbecue-chip bag, the big size, flapping away in the sage that grew to the door. Toward the house, a cat was curved over the wheel of the manure-spreader, staring for mice in the shadows under the box. And there was a sprinkler whirling on a yellow stool out in the garden; he supposed it must have run all night. It had taken Lucien nearly a month to make it from the county courthouse to here, an hour's drive. Lucien's unexpected appearance at Emily's hearing had been their longest and most intimate time together in all those years.

Lucien pressed the door shut on the sedan. There were willows alongside the garden, and birds continually speared down from them into the berries. There were numerous signs she was taking care of the place. He had put all he could borrow into making her bail; so these small sedentary indications were important. Still, it would take more than that to assure her being around on trial date.

The heat wave had gone overnight into the first edge of fall; the Crazies had come out of the shimmer and stood clear and separate above the foothills. Lucien was going to be there until the trial in late fall. He had an assortment of sporting trifles and equipage: rod, rifle, shotgun and a small pointer bitch curled in the sedan, a dog perfectly trained for the silence of the high plains hotels he had frequented. Such hotels exclude the barking, ill-mannered dog, some any at all. For the latter, Lucien had prepared the dog, Sadie, by teaching her to travel short distances, silently, in the bottom of his duffel. Her reward was silent dancing behind the locked door of the room, for high-protein baby snacks from the grocer. Watching her soar amiably past the television and the cheap furniture for midair interceptions of miniature sausages always prepared Lucien for the long sleeps he required to stalk the plains by day. It consoled him as his solitude deepened.

Lucien realized the hired man was looking at him. He must have been thereabouts all along, as he came up past the log chicken house with a border collie close at heel and silent. He was a tall man in his thirties with a mustache waxed off to points, and severely undershot boots. He was what they called around there "punchy"-looking —from cow-puncher, not punch-drunk. It was pretty clear he wasn't going to say anything. So Lucien told him who he was there to see, and he said about what. And Lucien told him that he had made Emily's bail. The man indicated the house.

Lucien must not have been comfortable, because instead of going directly to the house, he began to pile his belongings next to the sedan, as though he were going to move things indoors by installments. Then that was done and he put one foot in front of the other, clumped across the plank porch, thankful that the slant of morning light made the windows blank, and knocked. No one came, but Sadie appeared from the sedan and burned around the porch as though it were the lobby of a crazily permissive hotel.

31

He decided to look in a window. He put his fingers to the glass on either side of his face. It was not so much being able to see a little into the darkness, finally, as it was the sense of her eyes coalescing somewhere in that interior. He lifted a hand to wave and the eyes moved away. He knew she was at the door. When it opened, she said, "*My old flame*," in that deep voice from which laughter was never absent, even, apparently, in very hard times. At that moment Lucien was once again her suitor of all those years ago, probably as out of the question now as he was then, but as gripped as ever.

Her great dark looks had perhaps improved, especially to someone like Lucien, who liked crow's-feet in women almost above all other features. She was wearing house-painter's pants and a cowboy shirt with the tails out, and she was barefoot: she'd just gotten up. And how was Lucien different? He guessed he was losing a certain unreplenishable moisture. He went squirrelly after drink number 3 and resorted, in public places, to making a mark on his hand for each one; he never went out without a ballpoint pen. His craving for sport had become less a sign of buoyant youth than of crankiness and approaching middle age. In the nature documentaries that appeared on TV, he identified with the solitary and knowledgeable male, whether baboon or penguin; and this foolishness represented the same gap of wishful thinking that had plagued him all his life.

Emily's greatest change, obviously, was that she was under indictment for murder. As she opened the door for Lucien, he had the extraordinary sense that her eyes were somehow focused on his entrance while her thoughts were entirely elsewhere. Then she stared down at the dog, who backed about looking for a spot to sit:

nothing seemed quite right to her, and she stood crookedly next to the luggage. The luggage consisted of two tan bags from a broken set of smart luggage. When he'd been in foreign service, Lucien felt that luggage better identified the traveler than his own body.

"I'm, in effect, all alone here," said Emily by way of laying down her requirements. "There is the hired fellow. He's very nice and I don't treat him as a servant. Beyond that, he knows his limits. However, the feeling that I am living by myself is something I absolutely have to have right now." She was staring into Lucien's face and he was getting uncomfortable. He'd gone unchallenged for too long.

"Are you sure it's all right if I stay?"

"I wouldn't have suggested it otherwise. Besides, I obviously owe you one."

"Not at all, I—"

"Of *course* I owe you one. Let's not begin with baby talk."

Emily showed Lucien his room upstairs, and with mutual awkwardness they ferried his belongings there. He was briefed on the food, water and towel supply, and left to his own devices. Before going to the window, Lucien transferred his clothes into the dresser, stuck his Dopp kit on top and rubbed the heels of his hands into his eye sockets. Then he went to the window, where the feeling of cold mountain was in the light.

Lucien could see the trail and the gate the hired man had used from up here. There was an abbreviated bench of pastureland through which a creek threaded incandescent against wild grass. Then beyond were the Crazy Mountains.

Emily was moving around downstairs. Lucien kind of

tracked her at that as he tried to figure how the curiously separated range of mountains was attached to the earth. The heights of snow and light-relaying stone tied the range to sky as much as to ground. Anyway, he couldn't see how it was done, and he set his easel up without much hope, still hearing Emily's footfalls. At a certain age, seeing something is quite enough; breaking down those mysteries on another surface can be tiresome. Still, it seemed that trifling with paint was important.

Possibly Lucien's eyes would open to the stony hills, the sage flats that sparkled in the morning, the thousand skies of a fall in the Crazies, once he learned why she had killed her husband. Lucien knew that he had to take a broader view than that she was single again.

He went down to the garden. It was a well-tended spot with leggy, hopeless corn and the broad leaves of squash making a tremendous effort to yield a few miserable babies. It was too far north.

Lucien didn't see anyone moving around the yard, and there was no one on the porch or in the downstairs of the house. He was able to get his dog up to his room without using the suitcase technique he used at the hotels. She curled up under the bed and flattened her soft flews upon crossed paws. She understood this gambit instinctively. Lucien knew that in a pinch, she could handle the hunch-back stunt with the overcoat.

Lucien got back upstairs just in time, because once again Emily called him from the bottom of the stairs. When he jogged down, she said, "Come outside." Lucien went. Tied to the big cottonwood was a buckskin horse. "That's for you to use. His name is Buck and he needs shoes." The yard darkened in passing clouds, and Lucien saw the old buildings for the first time.

34

"The tack is in the partitioned half of the chicken house. Use my husband's saddle."

"I'm not going to try to paint today," Lucien said.

"Nobody expects you to!" A cruel, merry laugh followed her words, cause for thought.

Immediately Lucien began seeing the surface of the ground and the ranch buildings. Then the Crazies seemed to ignite upon the gloomy sky, something he had set off with his own fuse. But it wasn't quite enough. It had been only a month since he left Suzanne and James. He was still immobilized. He really wanted to paint because since boyhood he had associated it with peace and wholeness. In the Crazies the land stuck out in every possible way, and there was not much water visible. And rock. Lucien was really up against it; but Emily needed his help. It was all-important to preserve this sense of mission.

Lucien used to shoe his own saddle horses when he was a kid and could do it all day. Now he was merely neat, though the horse ended up standing square to the world and Lucien didn't swallow the nails. Buck's hoofs were the same color as the bottom of the draw Lucien could see from the bedroom and had transverse grooves under the coronal band that looked like the watercourses just below the snow line on the mountains. He had a good light source to shoe by and he was out of the wind. There were no flies.

Lucien saddled Buck and let him stand because he was cinchy and humped his back up. Then he climbed on and jogged him down the road, picked up the newspaper and came straight back up the creek bottom, right in the water, kind of floundering on the slippery rocks, approaching pools where trout fed on the projectile-clumsy grasshoppers. It was an old publicity stunt of the dude ranches to fly-fish on horseback for gullible mountain trout, a trick that had not lost its savor for Lucien; and he decided to bring some tackle for his next ride. Now he could look out through the tall wild prairie grasses on the stream bank and start to lose his sense of irony.

The telescope was on the kitchen table, secure in its tripod. It was early evening, and Emily and Lucien had their heads close together as they took turns looking at the wild goats crossing the granite ledge in the trembling mystery of magnification. There were five of them, and they moved in cautious flickers, dining on lichen and moss that only they could see. Their white was the purest opulent white, a yield from the surrounding mountains more absolute than an ounce of gold from a half million tons of gravel. One of the males stopped and looked into the deep vitreous lens, and his horns were fine and black as thorns.

"Is there anything you want from town?"

"No, but why do you want to go there?" he asked.

"I'm not embarrassed, if that's what you mean."

She took the truck, and when she was safely down the road, Lucien shot into her room for a bit of inventory. Stuck up in the edge of her dressing mirror was a photograph of Eric, her husband. He was wearing his surgical gown and hat, and smiled with blind triumph into the flashbulbs. Lucien thought of him undoing the strings of the cap and flinging forth the dramatic curls.

He's dead. Soon she'll love me again.

"Get your slicker and help me gather up some yearlings," said the hired man. Lucien borrowed a pair of spurs from a hook behind the door, and got a yellow slicker and a sweater. He got a pint of sour-mash and a hopeless little sketch pad. He got sunglasses and peanut butter. He didn't bring Sadie because he didn't want her hunting unless he was going to shoot, and he didn't want to get her kicked by a cow.

The hired man's name was W. T. Austinberry. He knew his job. The two rode for a few miles without speaking. Lucien happily remembered the ranch work of his school years. Though the sky was blue, Lucien kept expecting a storm because he could hear raindrops knocking upon the crown of his hat. Lucien mentioned the rain to W. T. Austinberry, who looked at Lucien like he'd been locoed. They rode on, and Lucien listened to the kind of heavy drops that portend a cloudburst, the sun beating down all the while. It wasn't until he removed his straw hat that he realized he had inadvertently trapped a few grasshoppers inside.

The two men ascended to the flat top of the first bench. They could look down from here and see the broad plan of the ranch with clarity, as well as the ascent of the agrarian valley floor to the imperial rock of the Crazies. The whole thing was forged together by glacial buttresses and wedges of forested soil that climbed until stone or altitude discouraged the vegetation. In springtime the high wooded passes exhaled huge clouds of pollen like smoke from hidden fires, which in a sense they were. These sights seemed to draw Lucien's life together.

W. T. Austinberry dogtrotted along with one elbow held out from his body like the old-timers one saw when Lucien was a boy. He had jinglebobs on his spurs, which tinkled merrily as he went. How Lucien loved this vaguely ersatz air of the old days! Or better yet, that the frontier lingered in these draws where Indian spirits were as smoky and redolent as the pollen exhalations of the forest!

They rode on and crossed a creek where W. T. Austinberry said that he had poured Clorox to kill a couple of hundred pounds of trout for his freezer.

"What was Emily's husband like?" Lucien asked nervously.

"He was a doctor."

"I know he was a doctor. I mean, what kind of a fellow was he?"

"Is it any of your business?" asked W. T. Austinberry. They rode a little bit farther.

"I guess I take it to be my business, or I wouldn't have asked." W. T. Austinberry stopped and stared at him like an owl. Lucien rode past him up the trail. "The husband, W.T., what was the husband like?" Lucien heard him click back into formation and come along.

"He had it coming," said W. T. Austinberry. He cut around in front of Lucien and pulled down a passing twig to pick his teeth with.

"Would a jury understand that?"

"Not necessarily."

The first bunch of yearlings jumped off the trail into a ravine and crashed through the underbrush like game animals. Lucien rode in pursuit, setting a suicidal course for W. T. Austinberry, who was obliged to follow Lucien through clouds of offended magpies, snapping branches and descending leaves until they turned the cattle against a wren-filled cliff and started their small herd on its proper course. Buck was a good horse who leapt off the rowel. He pinned his ears at laggard cattle and stole in for a nip. Lucien was excited to feel the horse's knowledge.

They were in a damp woods supplied by springs that stained the rocks and nurtured ferns, then brush, then trees. They found some cattle in there. The cattle stood with their legs sheathed in mud from the spring and watched their approach with the little gather they already had. The cows had mouths full of long grass but did not chew. W.T. and Lucien whooped them out onto hard ground and added them to the herd, and kept on moving. Lucien felt the distance of Emily's house, the height of the mountains, her endangerment from insult among the townies, and the strong autumn light that fell upon them and upon their horses.

The last bunch advanced out atop a thousand-yard avalanche of slide rock, innumerable pieces of shale that looked like they had just paused in violent flow, though their next move might have been a hundred years away. These cattle seemed to challenge them to come their way.

"Maybe we ought to look further on," said W. T. Austinberry. "We only need six more to make a pot." Lucien suspected W.T. had run out of guts; so he rode Buck out, floundering in pursuit onto the dangerous slide, and he soon turned the cattle back into the band. In a way, he was auditioning for Emily.

Buck was tired as they made their way down. He hung his head and they descended into thermals that held redtailed hawks like kites on rigid strings. He flung his big forefeet in lazy quarter circles and skidded slightly with his rear as they made their way through the changing air, and Lucien viewed the uniform backs of the flowing cattle with satisfaction. The old cows led the way like oxen on immigrant wagons. W. T. Austinberry dashed about returning the herd quitters, but they were on easy ground now and he must have known Lucien suspected him for a fool.

Emily came in with armloads of groceries, buoyant as a bride. Lucien had manure sprayed up to his shins from driving yearlings the last quarter mile down an alleyway alongside the pens. To him, unpacking the bags, the bright cans and bottles seemed in the old kitchen to be savage and modern and kind of exciting. The housewife on the laundry-soap box would have been taken for a prostitute at the time the kitchen was built. In Emily's cheer at these fresh supplies, she appeared dauntless; her indictment seemed to apply to someone neither of them knew.

"And now if you would—" she motioned him to the table, fanning contracts from a broad envelope onto its surface. She had already signed them and there was a dotted line just for Lucien. He scanned through and got the drift: Lucien owned the ranch if she jumped bail.

"For some reason," said Lucien, "I don't like the feeling this is giving me."

"The feeling this is giving you isn't the point at all. You had to borrow that money."

"Tell me what the point is, Emily."

"A fair arrangement between adults."

"I don't want a fair arrangement between adults," said Lucien. "I want a heartfelt gesture." He tapped his fingers on the tabletop without letting the nails hit.

"You won't get one from me," she said. "You'll get an arrangement."

"Where do I sign?" Lucien said with a flagging spirit. He was losing his self-sufficiency by leaps and bounds. Once in college when Lucien's roommate had kept a picture of his sweetheart on the drawer, Lucien had proudly displayed a framed photograph of his own hand. But now he had an uncomfortable sense that he was circling downwind of his best instincts. He sort of didn't like that. Lucien's nicest side was ruining his life. He signed the papers, and the distance from him to his wife and son was suddenly greater. It seemed he was never quite under control unless he was angry.

"There," she said, "I feel much better." She had her off-center smile, and the distant cast of her eyes which was not romantic or faraway but otherwise occupied. The smile brightened and the eyes focused on Lucien with a sexual glaze.

"You're still carrying that old torch for me, aren't you?" she asked with some pride.

"Yes."

"Why, how nice for you," she said. "To have a life's theme. An old flame. An old flame that never dies is like those overbuilt goddamn English shoes rich ladies used to wear. The illusion of everlasting life. That's what came with them. You buy a pair of those beauties when you get out of Miss Whozit's, and forty years later they haul you to the boneyard in the same brown shoes with the shiny eyelets. That's about how much the old-flame number is doing for me."

"May I have a blow job?"

"Pure poetry, Lucien. . . . I met a couple at Alabama Jack's restaurant in Florida who said they ran into you in South America. They said you had a wonderful wife, a beautiful girl, but you were inattentive to her and looked like you wanted to join the space program."

"I joined the USIA. Wasn't that enough for them?"

"Apparently not. They were absolutely sober."

41

Lucien scratched at the dial of his watch with a fingernail. "Look," he said, "is it all that terrible that I've gone on having these feelings? Not everyone has such a happy view of his own past."

"Was I the first girl you ever slept with?" she asked with terrific glee.

"Pretty darn close."

" 'Pretty darn close'!" She was put out. "How far did I miss by?"

"There was a real sweet Assiniboin girl at Plentywood when I was on the baseball team."

"It seems you have an array of genuinely happy memories," Emily said with unconcealed indignation.

Lucien raised a cautioning finger. "Remember, now, you were sleeping with the doctor. My dear."

"That guy," said Emily. "Don't worry about that bastard. I shot him dead."

•—•—•—•—•—•—•—•—•—•—•—•—•—•—•—•—•—•—•—•—•—•—•—•—•—•—•

The saw-whet owl, an occasional predator of the river lowlands, burned through Lucien's view and got something past the granary. There was a small cry, and it wasn't the owl's. Lucien walked and puffed on a bait-shack-style corncob pipe, a Missouri meerschaum he'd bought on a stateside trip with his aunt. He had been away from the area for years, some years in which English was his second language. He was an iron man of information, but just maybe what passed for strength of character was nothing more than a low resting pulse rate.

Using the corncob pipe as a prop, Lucien imagined himself old and alone on the ranch. In front of the frame house a piebald domestic duck cruised by itself on the green pond. Inside, an old man (the Lucien of the future) felt himself cooling, felt the heat of the light bulb on his hands as he turned the pages of his book.

Lucien started to get nervous.

That night the hired man had him down for ice cream and checkers. Though he scarcely knew him, Lucien played as though his life depended on it. Lucien knew W.T. took his frenzy for the creaking of a harsh and unremitting soul, but he played on.

Twice Lucien got up and stared at the lights of the main house. The third time W. T. Austinberry said, "Jump, and king me."

Lucien sat down and pressed three fingers on a checker he wasn't sure he'd play. He was suddenly afraid of something. Maybe he was just tired.

"Let's finish this game."

"Not till she's over," said W.T.

Lucien floundered onto his elbows. "Can't play any more." He was drunk.

"You gettin' you a little up to the big house?"

"Don't start that."

W.T. threw his head back. "Lord!" he bayed. "It's a little bitty world."

They fought bitterly but briefly, bloodying each other's faces on the floor, then refilled their drinks and resumed the checker game. The checkers were all over the board.

"You with the FBI?" asked W.T.

"'No, the USIA."

43

"Hunh. Thought she said the FBI. Thought you was a Federale."

"King, king, king!" Lucien splattered the checkers good. "I win, you lose . . . talk that way about my girl, you—"

"When's the last time you had a date with Emily?"

"What's it to you?"

"Go on, tell me."

"Years and years ago."

"Son, she's changed since that time." W.T. laughed deep in his throat.

"How?"

"She's a better shot," said W.T. with a wide cowboy smile. Then he grew alcohol-pensive. "This time I'm thinking about, I was trying to prove up on a lease I had over at Kid Royal. And we was getting ready to load out at Deadrock. I had the heeler up front with me, the radio on, when I threw a recap right on the scale. I was with Boyd, and he cusses and dumps a set of dead batteries from his hot shot, throws it in the jockeybox and said he's got a come-along to get our outfit to dry ground with. This was supposed to be the last of a big run of yearlings. And it turns out we got a five-hole spare for a six-hole rim. I knew right then and there my luck was shot. I knew them yearlings would bring next to nothing. God, it was bad. Also at this time I had a girl name of Shawna who wore a mood ring which was always nearly black. She cooked at the brandings and made eyes at the ropers. She was dumb. She read love comics and used her Chapstick as if it was a cigarette, and she was about as dumb as a stick. She lived at Parade Rest Trailer Park, which is no more than a breeding pen, and she was stick-ass dumb. But right about *then*, I met ole Emily. She come into the

sale yard and bought that set of cattle. She gave me my
break, and I ain't looked back since. She liked me."

"I can't tell you what this story does to me."

"I'd follow her to the gates of hell."

"That's her most famous effect, all right."

Lucien refilled the drinks while W.T. talked. "You
gotta make them women happy. Plow 'em, take 'em on a
trip, put a little smile on their lips. They like to spend,
spend, spend. So what I say is, let 'em." The thermostat
on the baseboard heater turned on and forced W. T.
Austinberry to get up and go a good part of the way
across the room.

He lay out on the floor, barely moving. Then it got
quiet. "Hundred-proof whiskey is a cowboy's color TV,"
said W. T. Austinberry from his own world on the bunk-
house floor, and passed out. Lucien looked at him: he
could no longer be reached.

Lucien had an awkward time getting back to his room.
He thanked W. T. Austinberry for the lovely evening,
then did the hurricane walk across the yard from tree to
tree until he achieved the main house. He did his best
going up the stairs, whereupon Sadie began barking at
him in sharp yelps. He smothered her against the floor
long enough for her to recognize him, then dragged her
into bed.

"*Lucien, what's going on there?*"

Lucien froze, clutching his dog. He heard Emily start
up the stairs. Then she appeared, eclipsing the dangling
bulb that threw a circle of electrical light around her.
She glittered in vengeful beauty.

"What've you been doing?"

"I'm afraid we got damn well good and drunk," said
Lucien.

45

"You and W.T. . . . ."

"Yes."

"What'd he say?"

"About what?"

"About anything."

"God, I don't know," said Lucien. "We were playing checkers."

"Let's take a walk."

"Let's take a walk!"

"Yeah," she said. "By the moonlight."

"All right," Lucien said and got out of bed fully dressed. Sadie shot repeatedly in the direction of the door, indicating her readiness for some hunting.

"Why don't you leave the dog . . ."

Lucien thought about it, then hitched Sadie to the leg of one of the ruined chairs and got a coat. Emily had a pair of jeans pulled on under a nightshirt. She tied the tails of the nightshirt and, downstairs, pulled a loose sweater over that. They headed into the night like laundry.

Lucien didn't feel very good. As they walked out into the dark, things rose to meet him, then passed. He once reached up to put an arm around Emily but missed completely without her noticing; his arm merely fell through air, then returned to his side.

Lucien made a willow-leaf mouth whistle and blew two notes over and over until Emily took it away from him. She led him over a ridge and a ravine and kicked to dust an abandoned anthill. When Lucien passed a big cottonwood tree, his shadow shot up the trunk, scared him, and disappeared.

In a depression between two small hills was the blue hole. Lucien had seen it before. It was a small steamy

46

spring, pouring hot water out of rock slab, then brimming over into the woods below. You could see the stars above and the lights of town beyond. Lucien reached down to touch the water, to see where the surface was. The only way he knew his finger had arrived at its surface was by the mark of current that appeared and shone in the light; and down below were shapely round stones that were deep and far away.

Lucien heard Emily's plunge, then saw her emerge through the curtain of bubbles, wavering like an inverted flame. Lucien left his clothes on the bank and slid in thinking, Now it's before I was born. They finned and treaded water in each other's arms. Emily took Lucien and got him inside of herself. She held him on either side of his head with the flats of her hands while they made a queerish love with nothing to hang on to. Lucien came out of her just at the end, and a jet of sperm spiraled to the surface and floated. Emily trailed it off with the tip of her finger and smiled at Lucien.

"It's been a long time," said Lucien. He felt himself rocketing into the past.

Emily dug her nails into the backs of his arms. "Just what did that sonofabitch tell you, anyway?" she said.

●–●–●–●–●–●–●–●–●–●–●–●–●–●–●–●–●–●–●–●–●–●–●–●–●–●–●–●–●–●–●–●–●–●–●–●–●–●–●–●–●–●–●–●–●

Emily had incomplete use of her hands from an accident she'd had some years ago in which her husband had figured. Emily was a talented pianist, and there had been this accident. Even when they were in high school she had been considered very gifted;

beyond just high school in Montana. They'd all expected to hear something of her talent, and then came this news of her getting her hands mangled. Lucien used to go over to her house and she'd be practicing. He had a brief, luminous spell as her sweetheart, ended, as it often was, by the arrival of Emily's future husband, the doctor. He was rugged, intimidating and athletic. He was probably about twenty-one at the time, but to Lucien he seemed to be some outlandish oldster like a millionaire or a Green Bay Packer. Lucien was nervous for the short time that he was around him, shuffling in the front hall of Emily's house. She and the doctor were soon a hot item. After that, that is, down through the years, the few reports were not good. Her husband was a surgeon, a hard drinker, a big-game hunter, a man of wealth; and so far as Lucien could tell from rumors and long-range snooping, tough with Emily. On a hot day she blew his brains out at close range and turned herself in to the sheriff in Deadrock.

This ranch had been meant as a kind of retreat for that childless couple. Since it was her neck of the woods—he was a Detroiter—Lucien guessed this meant a small capitulation for him. She came earlier each summer, but he never stayed past antelope season. Lucien had observed him a few times at the Bozeman airport, standing next to his luggage in a stadium coat arguing with the baggage handlers about his rifles. Lucien hadn't seen Emily at all.

But for a short time long ago, Emily and Lucien were going into the sunset as a composer and a painter, leaving the world a richer place. Within a few years he was distributing leaflets to Latinos for the U.S. government and she was getting knocked around regularly by her college sweetheart. Lucien had spells of delicious blind ambition, spells of painting, spells of high courtship and long, accompanied starlit walks on empty Western Hemisphere beaches, barefoot and with the pantlegs of a well-cut tropical suit rolled higher than the warm breaking waves. He married the companion and had a wonderful little boy.

He was sure Emily had had some fine times too. Lucien was now years older than that man she left him for.

Lucien attempted over the next few days to have a serious conversation about the cattle with Brer Austinberry. He was not interested. This place, he reminded Lucien, was a strict grass outfit and, as such, subject to the worst statistics then current in the cow business. There was a three-year immediate history across the state of Montana of beef prices dropping twenty cents per pound between turnout and shipping in the fall, which meant every cowman went backward until about halfway through the summer or maybe longer, depending upon the nature of his loan. This did not hold Austinberry's attention; he continued to jingle back and forth across the kitchen in his big roweled spurs. Lucien said, Let's haul everything to town this fall, accept that we had little that would grade better than utility cattle; then start anew with first-calf heifers in the spring. That meant buying some hay right away.

"We don't want to buy hay," said Austinberry. "We don't want to spend any money."

"What are we going to feed in the spring?"

"I don't care what we feed in the spring."

"Don't you plan to be here?"

After lunch he went up the dry creek bed that wound straight up to the Crazies like a holy road. There was an old wagon track that made parallel grooves in rock. In a hairpin turn he found a moldering pile of empty .45-.70 cartridges, an old firefight in a quiet hollow. Because of his hearty lunch Lucien was suffering what the nutritionists call the alkali tide, and in his lassitude he dreamed of water galloping down the rocky walls of the dry bed and taking him to the ocean, where no decisions would be required and where he could have his little boy back.

Lucien and the lawyer hovered around the glow of the lamp, a medieval gimmick in a lonesome theme restaurant, and a terrific minor anomaly for a Montana cow town. The lawyer, Wick Tompkins, was a heavy man who, you could see, had risen from another station in life. In trying to express the solitude of his existence, he asked Lucien if there was anything sadder than returning home to an empty answering machine. He had a quick-moving face that tapered cleanly from temples to chin; but his hands were those of an honest laborer and fell upon the table with an earnest thud to underscore each phrase. Lucien rather liked him, but Tompkins was determined to maintain an adversary air. It was he who had designed the ranch-forfeit document for Emily.

"She's going to go to the penitentiary," he said. Thud. "To make a long story short." This time the hands fell from a greater height.

"And you're her lawyer," said Lucien, raising his eyebrows.

"I'm her lawyer." The hands lay conspicuously still.

"Oh boy."

"Hey, look at it this way: she killed him deader than a mackerel. But this is the land of Japanese horseshoes, Taiwanese cowboy shirts and Korean bits. Who knows what a jury will say?"

"There must have been a reason she killed him."

"There was a good reason. He beat her. But he hadn't done it in a long time. Therefore it was premeditated murder. *She* describes it as premeditated murder. A jury with a room-temperature IQ will see it as *premeditated murder*. It's perfectly inescapable. Put yourself in my shoes. I'm going to explain how he slammed her hands in the car door to keep her from playing the piano. And about the time that sinks in, here comes Mr. Prosecutor with a photograph of the mortal remains featuring a face that's all powder burns except where the bullet actually goes in, which is a hole."

"Well, then," Lucien asked, "what good are you?"

"I am going to try to reduce her sentence, string out the road show through appellate court, work on her eligibility for pardon and just all-round obfuscate justice like the good mouthpiece I am. You know, for a country boy."

"I see."

"No, you don't see. What you see is acquittal for her and a fresh start for the two of you. Y'know, quiet evenings around your paint-by-numbers kit out there to the ranch."

"You're getting a little loose-lipped now. This thing is bad enough without the grandstanding. I mean, spare me. And make that your last one—" Lucien pointed at his drink. "Tank towns know few more unpleasant eyesores than native-son lawyers with land-grant educations tottering out of some roadhouse where they know the owner. . . . I got to go."

He started to leave. The lawyer called after him, "One'll get you ten you lose the hundred thou."

When Lucien looked back, the lawyer had a light sweat from thinking up his last line. It was like a jog around the block for a guy who runs a lot. He looked fairly pleased with himself, but Lucien appreciated him: freewheeling hick-town wise guys were getting scarce.

Lucien tried to think directly about Emily shooting her husband, a brutal Type A personality who took it out on all and sundry. Emily would look the facts in the eye. Lucien felt he had never been able to do that. He could see her weighing the old husband in the scales of justice the way a park superintendent reviews the record of a garbage-raiding bear who is scaring the campers: we've got one here who's got to go.

Lucien got up early and made breakfast. It was a wood stove with a water jacket, and kind of amusing to run. It had a lot of hot spots on top, so cooking eggs required moving the skillet around until you found a reasonable temperature that didn't burn them up. Today they were going hunting.

Lucien stole some glances attempting to see storm clouds on her brow as she ate. There weren't too many storm clouds. She still had the serenity of the class beauty transported through years of tribulation like a vase that has survived a revolution. It seemed a handsome contrast to his infuriating jauntiness, the air of boyish resilience that had probably cost him Emily in the first place. An eighteen-year-old boy with the air of a tired salesman thirty years his senior will get all the girls every time.

When they started out of the kitchen, Austinberry appeared and asked, "Where's everybody going?"

"Hunting," said Emily.

Austinberry stared at them for a long time, a gaze that was meant to be burning, and said, "Oh goody."

They stopped the truck at an old homestead. Lucien let Sadie out to tear around the buildings while they looked through the broken windows; all the glass was on the floor. There were worn-out irrigator boots and a Scotch cap hanging on a nail. The place had been empty a long time. There was a tin of bag balm on the sill that was heavy enough to be full, but the lid was rusted shut. The gray outbuildings surrounded a common space, and the sense of their being huddled against terrific and frightening outside forces was enough to make Lucien glad he had never faced the frontier. That was no spot for a guy who trips over his own feet.

The first field had been in years past a great one for birds. It was level and uniform, and the scent of fowl had lingered in its invisible air currents. A dog like Sadie would make a strong race and lock on point in the first two minutes. A wheel-line sprinkler lay across it like a monster.

"Emily," he said as they went along down the furrows, "how is it you're so calm?"

"I'm not calm. I'm fatalistic."

Lucien took this in. "You know I had a drink with your attorney."

"Oh, I wish that you hadn't done that."

"Well, I did, and *I* wish he were more optimistic."

"There's nothing for him to be optimistic about. He knows I'd do it again."

They hit a good stubble field. There was still frost on

it, and it looked like some huge glassy thing had tipped over and shattered. As Lucien looked across it to the Crazies, he wanted to shield his eyes. It was a beautifully farmed field that used all the flat ground; but it was wonderful to see the sage-covered remains of buttes and old wild prairie that wouldn't submit to plowing. Lucien released Sadie and she cracked off on her first cast, ignoring the showering meadowlarks that broke into song exactly as his bird book described it: "*Boys, three cheers!*" To Sadie these were mere decoration, furniture. The undertow of game was stronger.

For a moment Lucien didn't care whether Emily shot her husband, pissed up a rope or went blind. He had the sublime freedom of the hunt.

Presently they rode down among the thin, pale, jerky trunks of an aspen grove following a small stream toward its source. It must have been a spring because the stream's stable mossy banks were obviously undisturbed by run-off. When they reached the spring, it was just a swamp, a small and beautiful swamp, though, from which snipe bolted in that down-angled hurtling flight that makes them seem so bold. The wet ground supported an even, refined stand of cattails, some brown and velvety, some wound with streamers of windy cotton.

"These moments, these long looks," she said.

"How am I going to find any grouse without long looks?"

They had to go across some of the boggy ground. Sadie danced over the surface while they hunted dry spots and moldering logs. Once clear of the cattails and sedges, they could make out the shining granitic roof of the Crazies.

One of the miracles of the land was the isolation of water: as soon as they came out of the boggy ground they

54

were once more on the juniper and sage uplands, where the circulation of prairie air bore the feeling of distance and dryness and great shapes, quite different from the intimacy of spring bogs; it hardly seemed the two could exist side by side.

They followed a steep wash and, just below the line of wild roses at the crest, Sadie went on point. Lucien hoped the birds would hold, because it was almost a vertical climb. He started up, carrying the little L. C. Smith in one hand and looking for things to grab hold of as he went. He had to stop and blow like an old pack horse about halfway up; but she held the point, a brilliant mark on that ocher ridge.

Lucien arranged to come up on flat ground behind her and could see then that she was pointed staunch into ideal berry-filled cover. He was already anticipating the roaring flush. He glanced down to see Emily below him, watching with a slightly opened mouth. Lucien concentrated himself to shoot well, walked past Sadie to make the flush; but when the grouse went up he just watched them go, brown and mottled against the open sky.

• • • • • • • • • • • • • • • • • • • • • • • • • • • • • • • • • • • • • • • • • • • •

Lucien slept, and during the night he dreamed or overheard—he'd never know—incessant activity, activity which must have gone on long into the night: the dragging of objects over the wood floors, the random opening and closing of doors, the shunting about of vehicles in the dark, the long cry of a horse left in the wrong corral, then silence. When Lucien woke up, he found Emily awaiting him with breakfast on a tray. He was not warmed by this treatment and just leaned up on one elbow waiting for her to speak.

"It's all yours," she said, "but I'll always be able to come back, now, won't I?"

Lucien didn't speak. He guessed his accepting the knowledge she was leaving made him an accomplice. "I'd like a picture of you," Lucien said. "Portrait-style, with a good frame."

He watched the light and clouds make changes in his window; he saw the revolving shadows in the peaks of the Crazies, and night arriving not simultaneously but in different places and at different times. He began to wonder what screwballs lived here in other days who had hidden whiskey bottles under the porch or made the dog graves by the creek. Then having rested most of the day, he lay awake through the night and looked out the window at the cold moonlight on neglected meadows. He was just wondering how you'd care for a piece of ground like that. All that grass; all that timothy and brome and fox-tail and oat and fescue and rye and orchard grass and bluegrass and panic grass and river grass and six-weeks grass and brook grass! All those rocks! All that running water!

That night, aircraft lights wheeled around the flat across the creek and Emily was gone, a fading drone behind the clouds. Lucien wept at his loss. In these tears flowed the venom of a jilted schoolboy facing magic that wouldn't die at the right time and be good remembered magic.

The day broke on Lucien's ranch. He fed all the saddle horses because there seemed to be no sign of W. T.

Austinberry. He found himself unconsciously counting bales in the shed, dividing rations into the number of winter months. He stared at the shallow creek streaming through the corral and wondered where the best place to spud a hole in the ice would be. He also wondered if all those horses were indeed saddle horses or if there might not be a bronc mixed in there, disguising man-killer traits with good fellowship among the horses at the feed bunk. Then it came to him clearly: Austinberry had departed with Emily. For some reason it magnified Lucien's humiliation.

In W.T. he thought he saw a ridiculous version of him-self tottering off down the trail. And yet he peered with avaricious eyes at his own new land. He could only have seemed more preposterous to himself if he had been wear-ing a tie. He was spared that.

Well, Lucien thought, the sun goes down and the blues come around. He sat in the old chicken coop to get out of the wind and smoked and felt alone. He sat on a row of brooder boxes and watched the white and final streamers of cloud on the good sky. He had read somewhere that those are ice crystals, and at that time and place he felt they were. His whole past didn't shoot by, but some of the big items, the big wins and losses, did. By the time the harvest moon crossed the chicken wire, Lucien had looked at his life and was ready for a new one.

Lucien went inside; he filled the tub with deep hot water and soaked and watched the morning light cross the old linoleum flowers on the kitchen floor. He had benign thoughts for the man, now doubtlessly gone, who had dreamed up those appalling flowers for the linoleum factory. Could he have known what a half century's muddy boots and all that domestic abrasion would do to his bright flowers?

By the time early day in all its effulgence had pene-
trated to the bottom of the smallest gullies and sent the
dullest prairie chicken into hiding with a departing
hawk-warning cry, Lucien had climbed two thousand
feet above his ranch in an attempt to find out where he
was. He was beginning to understand what he had paid
to be here alone.

When Lucien was very young, he had read all
of the sporting magazines; and one of these, he
now remembered, had a feature called "This
Happened to Me," in which awful things happened to
sportsmen because of ice and cliffs and wild animals,
terrible things that the sportsmen survived by coming up
with something fast and at just the right moment. Or
they were saved by the inexplicable. For instance, the
polar bear sees his mate float past on an iceberg and
therefore releases your skull. This was very much like
divine intervention and was meant to leave you thinking
that it is the sportsman who is most directly exposed to
feeling the big flywheel, the eternal gear. What gave
"This Happened to Me" its special brimstone quality,
apart from the illustrations of sportsmen dangling, sliding or being pursued, was that each segment was signed
by the survivor. For a long time Lucien identified himself with these nearly anonymous men and began seeking
out ways of living that would produce civilian versions
of "This Happened to Me," combining the episodic, the
anecdotal yield and, best of all, the deep and abiding

smell of brimstone. When he tried to get away from that, he sensed nothing was going on; when he gave in to it, he found he required a steadily deepening effort in the episodes to produce a real "This Happened to Me" effect of sportsmen against the flywheel with a genuinely sulfuric atmosphere.

Now, sunk in consequences, he no longer wished that more would happen to him. Familiar remedies were not at hand. So he spent all his time out at the ranch, whose high pastures were shattered by ancient earthquake faults and brush canyons that turned upon themselves like seashells. Inside these canyons the sun or moon rose and fell inside an hour's time; a shadow would race at you like a guillotine. Insects were magnified in the angular light, and the rock walls seemed to have been cleaned with vinegar. Coyotes stole through the sequestered Byzantium, not knowing Lucien was there eating cold fried trout in these one-hour days which let him emerge into a larger day, feeling he had stolen time.

Lucien saw the sun move up toward him on the surface of the river. The river edged up in the bend as a cresting glare. His sedan was a luminous tear of terrific paint parked on the bank. If he rowed long enough, he would be tired.

He folded the oars within the gunwales and stepped out onto the bank with the bow line in hand. The drift boat ran off a bit on the eye of the current, then came to shore. He dragged the bow up on the cold pebbles and lit a cigar.

Lucien had taken the position that he was growing to meet himself, that he was ascending to a kind of rendezvous. He had placed himself on trial but would make the odd exception, because he had seen what little things break our parole from eternity. Last night's paper revealed that a man had been badly beaten, then shot to death guarding a Royal Doulton Toby jug collection. A quiet type met his end in a welter of porcelain and lead. Everything that meant anything was being sold to guitarists and pants designers. He was going to fish quietly and sweat it out.

Lucien and a new friend were finishing a long night together; they didn't quite know how. The road was warm. Birds had dusted in its course and disappeared once again into the brush along the creek. Aquatic insects drifted from the creek and speckled the windshield of the sedan moving between alternating panels of light, vegetation and sky. The sedan's luster was magnificent with nature's passing show.

"I'm going to shut it down here," Lucien said. The woman sat across the front seat just staring at him with a slightly swollen look about her lips. It was sunup, and her name was Dee.

Lucien lit a cigar and sighted around himself before directing its smoke toward the leafy staggered shadow from which the movement of cold water could be heard. He felt himself speeding up.

"Maybe I can catch a fish," he told Dee and got out. He strung the line through the guides of the rod and stared at the brushy enclosure through which the moving water announced itself.

"There's bugs," she said from inside, her head displayed on the wiper arcs. "Now they're on the dash. Can I play the radio while you do that?"

"Go ahead. Try and pick up the news."

Blue duns drifted over the tops of the willows. By the time he waded to the spring, he could no longer hear the radio. He caught four small cutthroats before turning his attention to the end of this small escape. He thought, I have only myself to blame. He closed the lid to the compartmented English fly box with its hundred treasures, and the escape was over.

"Did you get a fish?"

"I got three fish. Can you turn that thing down?"

"Three fish. That's nice. You got three fish. There, it's down. Happy?"

"Yes, very."

"That was a Top Ten crossover."

"You see, it gives me no special feeling. It's like being rolled around in a barrel."

"Uh huh. Y'know, I just imagine my old man's alarm went off about an hour ago." To Lucien daybreak had made her look like one of the monuments on Easter Island. "But here's the deal," Dee said, opening her compact, then throwing it back into her purse hopelessly. "Let's find a way to get this over with. My aunt will let me in through the garage. Nobody'll be the wiser."

Lucien started the car and moved down the road toward town. He tried to put some diplomacy and gratitude in his voice. "This sounds best for both of us," he said.

"You sickening fuck," she said. "I feel like a sewer."

The ranch house had a springy floor. Lucien's mother's house in town also had a spring to it. When Lucien was a child he could run through the first floor and cause the china to tinkle in the cabinets for a minute and a half. A train on the bridge would do the same; and the second-story sitting porch trembled at traffic or even, it seemed, the shouts of the neighbors from down the street. But this was a different motion, less the consequence of human pounding than some catarrhal moan from the ground, borne through the timbers of the house.

Part of the problem was that Lucien had got rid of the furniture. There was plenty of it, too. And behind the two mortifying unsprung beds there were hair-oil spots, but he thought, We've got plenty of haunts without this.

It was a heavy, windless fall of snow, a perfect day to burn furniture without fear of starting a grass fire. Wet and croaking ravens hung on the telephone wires, black and unassembled, like rags. He was drinking. He hauled the brutal beds, the all-knowing sofas, the crazed mechanical La-Z-Boy prototype which some solitary *Popular Mechanics* reader had put together and whose experiment Lucien made a shambles of. These, surmounted by chrysanthemum-print linoleum in quarter-acre lots, doused with number 2 diesel fuel, took only a match. The first lit up the fine, dense snow and produced the effect of sunny fog; anything at a middle distance—horses, trees, fences—shone through with an intense gray like spirits banished from the furniture. It did not seem then to Lucien as he paced around the draconic snow-licking flames with his bottle that there could be a way to call him unlucky; or upon consideration, to subject him to opinions of any kind. He was lying to himself.

The bedroom was empty of everything except what would furnish a dormitory room; the vacancy seemed more rueful than the furniture had. And there were bullet holes in the mystery circles of hair oil. But nobody is improved by having his child taken away. Today it was official.

·   ·   ·

The sound of snow slumping from the barn, the chinook winds at night, coyotes below the house competing with noisy ballgames on the television, wood smoke and the moan of tractor engines, serious flotation of the river in his drift boat, generally good behavior if you omit one five-hundred-mile blackout on the interstate. Which nobody got wind of.

Dear Herbert,

I have been made aware of your and your client's version as to why I would like to see my boy before winter and why I would like to see his report cards, school projects, drawings and so on. I am made to understand that you and your client imagine that I am building some sort of case to reverse a decision which I have with some considerable difficulty learned to accept. I am further led to believe that you have encouraged your client in this kind of thinking.

Herbert, I must assume that this is a false idea; and that whoever generated such a diseased piece of reasoning has either the ability to correct his thinking or the common sense to recognize that people who are wronged seek whatever remedies that there are available to them.

I know you will understand what I am saying.

Sincerely yours,
Lucien Taylor

Wick Tompkins had his small low offices across from the monument to the fallen cavalryman, a grimacing bronze fighter already dead, falling on an already dead horse, seizing the shaft of the arrow that pierced his tunic, suggesting that the last man still left alive in the world was the bowman. Wick liked to point out that the chap would have had to be standing somewhere right close to his secretary's desk when he got the trooper.

Since Emily's departure Wick and Lucien had become friends.

The secretary winked up from her new data processor, then rolled fresh boilerplate onto the screen. This machine had made Wick a man of leisure: Wick now weighed two hundred forty pounds. He smiled all the time, and his smile said, This better be funny.

"Lucien, come in here and close the door. I don't want anyone to see you. Your hat, give me your hat."

Lucien reached his Stetson to Wick, who hung it on a trophy for the champion mare at the Golden Spike show in Utah.

"Herbert Lawlor informs me that you have threatened him with a letter."

"I did not. I wrote him a letter."

"I've seen the letter."

"So you know that Herbert Lawlor is hysterical."

"The letter has threatening overtones. It is a pissing fight with a skunk. It is the very thing you are not to do. You're having fun out on that crummy cow camp, aren't you?"

"I'm making repairs."

"And you are floating on the river?"

"Almost every day."

"I think that's grand. Especially if you let me do the communicating with Mr. Lawlor. It's demeaning for you to take these things into your own hands. I am paid to demean myself, though I dream of glory as well as weight loss and sex miracles with strangers."

"I'll do better at everything if I can see my boy."

"You will see him at Christmas, and you're going to have to get used to that."

"Christmas."

"That's the *next* time, not the *last* time."

"How do you know when the last time is?"

Wick Tompkins drew on his cigarette, made a tentative gesture to stub it out, decided that too much of it remained and said, "I think that is a disastrous remark."

"It's not a remark. It's what I think."

"It's a disaster."

When young girls learn the new dances, thought Lucien, it is the last time the new dances are interesting. I am in town, thought Lucien, why not make the most of it?

He sat down at the counter at DeWayne's Place, a hangout for people dramatically younger than himself, and drank coffee, the fastest beverage in the house. DeWayne's was an old soda fountain, in the same family since Eisenhower. Grandpa, Dad, Edd, Edd Junior, still there: a dynasty of soda jerks. He drank as much coffee as fast as he could and watched a two-by-four opening at the end of the room where the young girls danced together to a jukebox. Their movements were strange and formal, glassy and distant; and everything wonderful about their bodies was under twenty-four months old. They moved toward the bellowing music, then moved away, gazes crisscrossing. They arced toward the surrounding columnar tables and quick-swigged pop without losing the beat. Though much of this struck a deep chill in Lucien, part of him desired to be a shallow boy with a sports car. Anything he'd ever done seemed like old tickertape.

Lucien knew that he had to practice an upright existence. He was being watched, not by everyone as he imagined, but fairly closely watched. People seemed to think he was waiting for Emily.

When he emerged from DeWayne's, he felt as though his trousers were undone, or that his face and neck were a mass of hickeys. He saw two people he knew. One was the messianic Century 21 realtor, H. A. "Bob" Roberts. Bob cried out a greeting. He coasted past Lucien with a marathoner's stride, but kept his face locked in Lucien's direction.

The other was Mrs. Hunt, Lucien's mathematics teacher of years back. She had been retired for a long time and now stalked Main Street reproaching former students, some of whom were grandparents and had had quite enough of this from her over the years.

"Aren't you a little old for that place?" she asked Lucien.

"I guess I am," Lucien said, staring at a smile that revealed three quarters of a century of cold fury. "I'm kind of chipper when I'm in a spot like that. What d'you think?"

"We're talking about self-control, aren't we, Lucien?"

I ought to pound this geek, he thought.

It was the perfect setting. Lucien sat with Dee at the first table this side of the closed-circuit television screen, an immense thing which stood huge and pale in the dark room. Along the wall were dark, empty, intimate booths, and they seemed as infested with ghosts as Mexican catacombs. The bartender put so much shaved ice in the blender drinks that Lucien never knew why his head was numb and his wrists ached. All he had to go by was mood swing.

"What in God's name am I doing here with you?" she said.

"I couldn't guess." He stared in fear at his drink.

"Did I tell you how glad I was you were able to catch a few fish the other day?"

"No, you didn't, but thank you."

"So this is love."

"Well, it's very nice, isn't it."

"So this is your capital F love."

"No, frankly, it's not. But it has a nice side. Barkeep, may I have a black olive?"

"For your margarita?"

"Precisely."

The bartender arrived and dropped the olive from about two feet right into the sno-cone.

"Thank you," said Lucien, staring straight at him.

Dee was actually pretty, except that, to Lucien, her neck seemed a little strong, a little sculptural. A blue vein crossed it like something hydraulic. Perhaps if her head had been a trifle bigger . . . Then everything else would have been out of whack. Lucien had been through this before: change shoe size, hollow the ankles a bit along the tendon line, rotate the ass a few degrees north. After that you might as well load it out in a wheelbarrow.

"I ran into my old math teacher. She was cruel and made me feel old."

"I've got a good buzz now."

"I hadn't been doing anything wrong, and she kind of nailed me." Lucien watched her with a wary gaze.

"*Le buzz magnifique!*" Dee cried.

"So as to what you're doing here, I don't know and I don't care. This old broad made me feel like a bum waiting for his heart to blow up in some bus station."

She stared at Lucien for a long moment.

"Say my name."

"Oh, darling." Lucien felt panicky.

" 'Cause you don't know the goddamned thing, do you. What do you take me for, a Kleenex?"

Lucien made a smile. It looked right and understanding. It looked okay. He thought if dismounting were given the same importance in sex as it is in horsemanship, this would be a happier world.

"Stay right there," she ordered him. "Don't move."

She went to the bar and had a word with the bartender. He leaned on the hand that held a towel. From Lucien's distance, the bartender looked like Father Time. He blinked while she talked to him, nodded, wiped at the bar suddenly, and she curved on back to the table.

"Don't worry about a thing. I've got a late date with the bartender. He dearly loves to party."

"So everything's fine . . . ?"

"Yeah," she said, feeling in her purse for a cigarette. "Said it'd be about half an hour."

"*Dee!*" Lucien shouted, but it was too late.

A Kleenex. It was astonishing that she could make a remark like that, whatever her bitterness. Lucien, with not a little delusion, attempted to picture her husband, the background of the bitterness. Her husband belonged, by all Lucien could tell, to that class of people, usually vainglorious cuckolds, who chainsaw through trailer houses, use dump trucks for revenge upon their wives and girlfriends and are eventually captured, lambs with anomalous records, by baffled authorities, accorded treatment for stress and released into a new world.

Lucien drove up the valley. The purling creeks glittered in the hillsides. It is still heartening, he thought, that the water goes on going downhill.

So he launched his drift boat again. He floated and

smoked between the chalk cliffs. For a couple of hours he let the river take him away, toward the bubble of the ocean, toward teeming populations with women who looked like they came from Egypt, who did not seem to have been raised on pancake mix. For a while he felt the nation and its people coming to him, and then he dragged the boat out on a gravel bar, spooking eight fledgling ducks whose takeoffs failed. They pinwheeled into the reeds and disappeared.

I am a family man, thought Lucien, despite what has been stolen. He persevered in viewing himself as a victim.

Please send one tall bottled spirits of oleander. The north wind is tearing this joint up. Please send one sentimental war memorial heated by the sun and suitable for emplacement on coastal Bermuda grass. Am anxious to review above-captioned properties with canal and floating coconuts as pistol targets. Guard dog an unnecessary extravagance, also dismantle hydroponic tomato system as I am in all respects devoid of a green thumb especially as it applies to my own life.

Lucien thought, Possibly I should not have thrown out all the furniture. The wind has a bit of a run at things as is, don't you think? Of course it has. It's like being left in the barn.

He sat bolt upright in the cane rocker, an amber shooter of whiskey in his hand. The cruelest thing I did on my father's death was to request "no keening" of my relatives. We could start from there. Sixty-six years of his wreaking havoc did not seem an appropriate background for some loud Celtic attempt to grease the boy to heaven. I'll take my lumps; he'll have to take his. If he's going to heaven, it will have to be as an exemplary

69

criminal, a figure of pathos, there to give the chiaroscuro effect to happy souls who have everything.

As to my child, maybe I am doing no better. Perhaps I *should* deal with principals only, phone it in without too much English on it, looking at myself with the instrument to my ear in the wind-shuddering front window and ascending foothills enameled on the darkness. Punch in this Yankee-Doodle area code, digits falling through the computer. If I get a boyfriend, I'll sing "How's My Ex Treating You?" with castrato enthusiasm. Calm down.

"Suzanne?"

"Yes?"

"It's me."

"What time is it?"

"About eleven here. I can't see my watch."

"Huh. One here. What's up?"

"Are you having company?"

"What's up, Lucien?"

"I'm afraid I've been rude to your lawyer."

"Oh, so I'd heard. You're going to have to stop that."

"I have already. On advice."

"Where are you?"

"I'm out at my ranch."

"What time did you say it was?"

"Almost nine."

"Huh. Must've dozed off."

"Where am I?"

"What?"

"Where am I?"

"Lucien, I'm sure if *you* don't know—"

"Remember years ago, New Blue Cheer?"

"Yes—"

"They still make that stuff."

"All right, pal. That's enough."

"I was playing our old tune, Suzanne."

"What was our old tune?"

" 'My Girl.' "

"This is news to me."

"Anyway, I listened to it and it was good. It was clear and it was good."

"Okay."

"I demand to see James."

"You will have to demonstrate to a neutral party that you are worthy."

"I ought to brain you."

"See what I mean? Besides, you're in a completely other time zone. So that is a sick fantasy. It would be ill enough if you said it to my face, but this is ill-on-ill. And every time you light into my attorney, you look slightly less good to neutral parties."

"Am I to understand that I have to get a gold star from every pot-licker who cares to evaluate me or I don't see him?"

"That's probably the best way for you to view it. James is not something that you picked out of a litter. He is a little person entitled to the usual assortment of human rights. It's my job on earth to see that he gets them. It's also my job to be at work in about seven hours. It's not nine o'clock. Not here, not there. Not anywhere. I'm going before you get your tail into a worse crack than it's already in. Goodbye."

She hung up. There was no smack of black plastic, just the buttons going off, a regular hangup. Lucien could tell he had not particularly gotten under her skin. Then suddenly he was clear. What he had done had made it a

71

little harder for him to see his child. It had been a long day and now it was over.

He called back.

"Sorry."

"Okay, I accept, goodbye."

Lucien put on his coat, went outside and felt for the porch rocker.

He sat in the dark with his hands in his sleeves and looked at the grayish silhouettes of cattle along the creek. He startled some bird when he first moved in the rocker, and the papery awkward rush of wings near his head made him nervous. All of him seemed out of the moonlight except his shoes, which shone disconnected before the rocker. He moved his eyes from the knuckles of his left hand to the knuckles of his right hand. There was a little light on them. I'm still here, he thought.

Before his father had died and he had asked everyone to refrain from keening, in fact many years ago, Lucien had gone on a fishing trip to the Bear Trap on the Madison River with his father, a man named Ben Rush and a man named Andrew McCourtney. Each night his father and Ben Rush would go to the bar and tell fish stories, then come home and pass out till halfway through the next morning. They'd wake up and tell fish stories right through their hangovers, which they would cure with bourbon chilled in the icebox. Andrew McCourtney was a fragile Irishman who had been shell-shocked, and his face had sudden unwilled movements. McCourtney seldom drank because it threw him into the Second World War, and he'd screech about booby-trapped German cameras, snipers in bombed châteaus, and law school: he'd flunked his bar examination and become a salesman, working for Lucien's father and Ben Rush, a former prizefighter from Chicago.

So McCourtney got up early while the other two slept, and awoke young Lucien to take him out for the morning mayfly hatch; and Lucien would be completely and unquestionably happy.

Lucien's father and Ben Rush liked to play tricks on McCourtney, and one night they took Lucien aside. Here's a good one, they breathed on him: when McCourtney comes round in the morning, tell him you're not in the mood to fish; tell him to find somebody else. Lucien lay up long after the two came crashing in, worrying about the joke. He assumed at least that his father knew what he was doing. So when McCourtney came to the door, he piped, "I'm not in the mood to fish. Find someone else." And McCourtney was gone.

He waited around the camp until his father and Ben Rush woke up and told them he had delivered his speech to McCourtney. Neither of the men could remember how it began. When McCourtney came back to camp with his rod and a full creel, Lucien hurried to explain the joke. "That's all right, Lucien. We leave tonight." But McCourtney was no longer there, not in his bright twitching expectant face of the early morning, or in any other way. His remoteness lasted Lucien indefinitely.

Tonight on the windy porch, features of the darkness began to emerge to his adjusting eyes. He thought, I wonder if this is it. He considered his child's decent circumstances. I couldn't do as good a job, he thought, and went inside for a drink. Find somebody else.

When he awoke, he could hear car engines starting just past the curtains. He didn't know where he was. He went to the window and looked out upon a parking lot and beyond to the jerky movement of early traffic. He sat on the edge of the bed, picked up the phone and dialed the desk.

"What's the name of this place?" he asked.

"It's the El Western," said the voice. "This is the El Western. May I help you?"

●-●--●--●--●--●--●--●--●--●--●--●--●--●--●--●--●--●--●--●--●--●--●--●--●--●--●--●--●--●--●--●--●--●--●--●--●-●

A great blue norther made up and came down off the High Line. Lucien went into town and bought some duck loads for his sixteen-gauge. He admired the town for its symmetry in the bend of the big river, for its smoky cheer in the face of this raid of arctic weather. Then he went off and hunted ducks in a place where a spring creek, having arisen in one small eye of a swamp, wound out in a long ribbon of steam toward the river a couple of miles away. He walked along while the deep cold made a bas-relief map of his own skull, exposing bone through flesh and reminding him that cold, not heat, is the natural order. Suddenly his small white frame house seemed a pale, brave island in eternity. A more analytical person might have concluded that this solitary regimen was a good and happy one for him. But he was old enough to know that loneliness, like some disturbance, would begin to form.

The ducks jumped straight up through the steam with a hard electrical wing-beat, and Lucien shot a pair of drakes. Green-headed and orange-footed, they were northern birds so heavy as to seem like small geese. Lucien broke open the gun, and the empties jumped smoking onto the ground. His overworked tear ducts made his eyes blur from the warmth around the spring. He sat and plucked the birds, an easy job with their still-hot bodies. Down drifted and caught in the russet brush, and in a short time he had a pair of oblate units of food, the meat shining pinkish through a layer of creamy fat and pale dimpled skin. Lying next to them in the snow were the matched green severed heads. High above Lucien, one flight after another, long stringy Vs seemingly in the stratosphere, headed south. Lucien looked forward to his dinner and could not avoid realizing that these two weren't going.

He put his ducks in the front hall and stood the shotgun in the corner, all without taking off his coat. Then he went back outside and started trudging toward the curl of smoke a couple of miles away that marked the neighbor's house. He had to make some friends. Maybe the neighbor liked ducks. The movement of his legs in the light snow reminded him of a mild ocean breaking on a gradual sand shore. He remembered bobbing in the ocean at his uncle's Oregon house, rising to view the beach, then dropping again to let his boy's mind run wild with the sense of being lost at sea; a few strokes and he would come breaking out of the surf onto the warm beach where his beloved cousins played.

Instead of his cousins and the sea, thirty years were gone, and he made his way to the bitter stone-and-clapboard home of his neighbor. The neighbor was working on a front-end loader next to a Quonset shop. At all its moving junctures grease and debris had frozen; they were frozen to the consistency of taffy now, and the neighbor was chunking the stuff away with the end of his screwdriver. He didn't look toward Lucien as he walked up. Lucien gave him his name and he nodded. In the silence a colossal ranch wife moved past the Thermopane window of the grim house and vanished.

"What's wrong with the loader?" Lucien tried.

"Don't work."

"I see."

Lucien looked over toward the corrals. There were small bunches of cattle spotted around here and there, and outside the corrals an unwound round bale that the neighbor could pitchfork feed from. The fork was stuck straight up in the center of the bale. Lucien was unable to think what he might say to administer some routine welcome.

"Anyway," he said. "I just decided to stop down and, y'know, say hello. My name is Lucien Taylor." The neighbor, Jerrold Carpenter, said absolutely nothing. "I'm your new neighbor." This time Lucien could make out the slight shrug under the brown coveralls. It meant "So?" A fine heat rose about Lucien's neck. He decided not to bring him any ducks.

"I noticed your half of the fence is in considerable bad repair," said Lucien. "That's going to change."

The man stopped prying sludge and looked at Lucien. "You're going to fix your share of the fence this year. If your cows get on my place, I'm going to move them on down to the highway and let them go. I also understand you've been greedy with the water. This year I'll see to it there's a ditch rider in June to teach you to stop stealing. I've got two hundred miner's inches and I'm going to get them. The last thing is, don't *ever* set foot on my place without permission. Pleasure meeting you. Goodbye."

Lucien trudged down the drive and started back to his place. He felt awful. He began remembering in amazingly vivid detail how he had come up with his dream of a life of foreign service so many years ago now. In the dream there had been the flow of words and ideas; there had been itchy feet and rambling fever. Much of this had evaporated against a background of dysentery and human rights violations, a background of vacant government pamphleteering on his own part; and the dribbling on-again, off-again attempt to make a family within an overpowering feeling of disconnection. Growing up in a small town, he didn't quite belong in land he knew and loved, and he no longer belonged in town. On the radio a young woman offered a broken refrigerator for sale. "Suitable for a smoker." A baby wept in the background.

Belong. What a word. Drives everyone fucking nuts, thought Lucien. You look at children and they belong where you drop them, while time only makes them lost. What a system. Cross that River Jordan, hoss, leave it all behind.

When he got to the house, Lucien went inside and called the neighbor. "Start ordering your materials," he said. "You've got a lot of fence to build in the spring." He sat at the kitchen table and blew power calls on a duck call he'd carved out of bois d'arc in shop class. He blew highballs and greeting calls and feeding calls. Sadie tilted her head and listened.

There was snow drifted low around the meter bases; and at the end of Main Street, the Absaroka Range, which seems to keep its distance in warmer weather, looked aggressively close. A woman shouldered her way out of a secondhand store with a table lamp; its shade angled suddenly into the prevailing wind and she backed all the way to her sedan with it in her arms. Her rayon scarf waved crazily.

Lucien wore overalls and a camouflage duck-hunting

coat. He tried saying to himself, There but for the grace of God go I, as each person passed him; but soon he detected that the gap was less clear than he hoped. He soon imagined they might have a better place to go than he did. Some of these people he knew had huge video dishes next to their homes and knew a lot more about Shiites and Druze militiamen than he ever would. I am absolutely lost, thought Lucien, I mean absolutely.

Winter came as a series of color extractions; Lucien dutifully painted the shrinking values. By March, one thing had become fairly clear: Lucien had no talent. Drinking and womanizing seemed the only solution. So, quite abruptly, he went from being the mysterious loner out on his ranch to a virtual town fixture and barfly. He learned to sleep on the jukebox. Frequently he took his lady companions back to the blue hole, where they played and soaked and crawled out onto the heated mud for drunken intercourse. It wasn't that pretty at all. Any attempt at a gay thrust only shoved your partner deeper into the mud. Grunting and floundering while all one's own limbs made sucking noises was, Lucien felt, a real icebreaker with the more timid gals. Lucien hoped to one day develop this spring into a spa. In April he had a close call when a brunette passed out in the mud and sank from sight. He had to probe for her with a stout pole to make the rescue, then load her to town with only her eyes showing: he had been afraid to let her rinse in the bottomless hot spring, for fear of not seeing her again. Though it would have been hard to notice then, she really had a great personality. Her father was Lucien's age; he met them at the door and beat Lucien to a pulp. That night Lucien slept at the hobo cave down by the river. He stared up at the dozens of red elk the Indians had made and remembered wanting to paint.

During the night it had turned off bitter cold; the anchor ice rolled down along the formerly blue channels and stacked up on the gravel bars, where they made glittering midday heaps. Lucien parked his sedan and let the motor and heater run. He looked down below the highway riprap into a deep pool where ice was actually growing from the cold bottom in low shining subaqueous domes. He remembered fishing near Boca Chica Key in Florida when the Navy was fueling its jets beyond the mangroves. There was considerable heat on the shallow water, and through the guano-covered vegetation one could smell hot jet fuel and asphalt. He pretended the noisy fanned heater of the sedan was the Southeast Trades and lit a cigar. When James was a very small boy, he and Suzanne had gone to Green Turtle Cay. Lucien remembered the three of them riding the ferry across Abaco Sound next to a stack of weatherproofed Last Suppers consigned among the island provisions for the Christmas trade. They walked along the main street of the town of New Plymouth beneath the string of domestic light bulbs that illuminated the street at night and listened to the singing of the choirs in the minute churches of the town. Lucien took James into the one-room abandoned jail, then took him climbing on the ancient, burst coral tombs with their decorative conch shells. The ladies went by in the winter heat holding tiny black Bibles and wearing lavish headgear indicative of a cherished life on earth where the warm sea makes man contented and stupid. Later, when all the gentle coasts had drawn the feel-good elements of society to their fragrant shores, Lucien would return to the frozen north for a bit of self-immolation, sacrifice and malfeasance. Still, the best thing of that year had been teaching James to open coconuts with a screwdriver, that in a year of great professional advancement and policy impact. He wasn't wondering how to get out. He wasn't thinking of rising above foreign service with a spy novel or a well-publicized dispute with Congress or the President. The coconut, the screwdriver and his son stood out above all other concerns, great and small. But his wife had come to seem kindly; and everyone knows how well that one does against the other woman. When Emily was indicted, Lucien was gone before he knew what had hit him. Later he would seem to go mad as his unconscious dealt him most of the blows he so richly deserved. Often a man displaying signs of seemingly crude suffering—drooling, crazy laughter, embarrassing public drunkenness—is actually, under the surface, suffering from something intricate; in Lucien's case, all those gossamer horrors that stole his happy home from him made of him something whose chain one pulled at one's peril. But he was growing calm; calm at first in defeat and in the drifting lethargy that defeat produces. With Wick Tompkins's help, though, there had come to be a stirring within. Maybe a big one to make a lie of all one's past errors.

"Suzanne, this is strictly a professional call. I need your help in a very specific way."

"Who is this?"

"This is Lucien," said Lucien with an unnecessary air of patience.

"What can I do for you, Lucien?"

"What are you wearing right now?"

She hung up and he had to redial and apologize, explaining that it was just a joke.

"I want to start a business with my hot spring," he said. "Nobody would believe in my idea. But you would. The others would take me for a crackbrain."

"You're right," said Suzanne, the kind of woman healthy men dream of. "I'd probably buy it."

"Suzanne! I want you to come back. I want you and James back! I'll do anything!" There was no hint of insincerity in Lucien's voice. "I can see clearly now!"

"Absolutely not."

He knew she'd say that, but he was distracted with sudden wild and sourceless yearning that rode right over the predicted rejection.

"Can we just try?"

"Lucien, I really don't think so. My famous optimism is gone. And let's face it, you haven't achieved a thing since you went back to Montana."

"That I don't believe."

"Besides, I'm no longer optimistic enough to feel lonely."

"You don't have to feel lonely. We can try again."

"What I'm saying is I *don't* feel lonely."

Lucien's heart and groin ached, all the right signs. He'd done well to take to the phone. But even Lucien riding the long swell of revelation could see this one had gone nowhere fast.

"It's still snowing!" he cried.

Another call yielded little more.

"You and me and James can have a beautiful life here. James could grow up on the ranch—"

"*That* ranch?"

"Yes . . ."

"Oh, Lucien."

Upon thought, it seemed a little early for issuing invitations even to Suzanne and his boy. Suzanne was right, he didn't have much of a record. But he went on feeling he could change that. He knew he had to.

Finally spring began to come, and with it, new merriness. New merriness sent Lucien down the road of vintage tequila; and that resulted in a hiatal hernia from throwing up. Sometimes now even well-chewed food seemed to get stuck before heading toward his stomach, a disconcerting thing. He'd read about well-off citizens choking on big steaks and dying in front of maître d's, and he didn't want to go that way. With his new merriness, he didn't want to go at all.

He was so excited and, really, agitated that he ended up with his former companion Dee. They took a cooler filled with ice and drinks and snacks, wonderful things that she had made with her own hands, and went to the drive-in movie, a fine old concrete thing that stood in front of the great mountains of the wilderness, playing to an amazingly small parking area on a spring night. It was such an early-day drive-in that it should have been one of the primary artifacts, alongside the buffalo jumps and Calamity Jane's favorite bar, of this good little town. When Lucien was learning to smoke, now among his most demeaning habits, he used to go up to the projectionist's chamber. The projectionist, a woman in her sixties, would draw out the glowing carbon rods from the projector and light Lucien's cigarette.

Now many years later he was parked again in this

lonely spot in a row of less than twenty cars. We've put a bad hurt on this cooler, thought Lucien, and now it's mostly gone. The car had become a very private place where Lucien went in and out of focus. He had long since quit trying to understand what Fred MacMurray was doing up on that screen, squinting down through his pipe smoke at a freckled redhead with a newsboy's sack.

The engine was running to keep their naked bodies warm, and Lucien could feel its RPMs registering through the seat cover. "It's too early to open a drive-in," he said. The reason why they were sitting at opposite ends of the seat was that Lucien had learned that Dee was having her period, and he was discouraged. Now and again he would tear his eyes from Fred MacMurray and look quizzically at the small trailing white string, trying to think what to do. She was not a little disgusted by his squeamishness. He felt like a touchy town kid confronted by his first lusty country maiden. And it didn't help when she indicated for him to come to her side, with the same gesture used by zoo bears asking for a peanut. Still, it was already clear he would have to come through.

He leaned over and cupped the heated weight of one breast. Then he kind of bounced over to her and got the string between his thumb and forefinger. At first it wouldn't come loose; then it came all at once and hung between them like a rodent. She wrinkled her nose and pointed sharply at the window. Lucien gave it a toss, but somehow the string and the thing's actual weight were such that it flew way too far and landed on the windshield of one of the other cars. Lucien stared over there in real fright. It was stuck right in the middle of the windshield. As Lucien watched, the wiper blade moved up and bumped it without moving it very much; the blade retreated and then moved upon it again, this time sliding it to the top of the windshield where, anyone could see, it was going to stay.

Then the door of the car opened up and a bruiser in a cowboy hat got out and began to look around. Lucien felt his organs shrink dramatically, an ancient prelude to flight. The big cowboy moved boldly from vehicle to vehicle staring into each one, quietly asking a few questions. When he was only one car away, Lucien felt he should engage the transmission. A moment later he shot away, spraying ancient drive-in gravel while the cowboy shouted, "I got my fiancée here! She don't want to know about your little world!" And in a short time Lucien was tearing along, bare and alert, while the golden lights of his car lit up the canyon south. "This is the life!" he cried. "They can have that Fred MacMurray!" It was the first movie he'd seen in a year.

The next morning was another thing entirely, another day that began with the query, Where am I? This time it was the ranch. Immediately he began to remember the events of the previous night; now of course they were devoid of the verve that actually made them happen. Lucien felt the heat of shame start up the back of his neck and then consume his entire face with the burning, prickling agony of remorse. Back somewhere in Lucien was a residue of puritanism that surfaced on mornings like these which would convince some of his enemies that he did in fact pay in the end. Lying in bed, with late-morning light on him, he thought the veins in his hands were too prominent, and his scalp itched. His previously clever mouth was a cup of variegated scum; and his poor old dick was a grim souvenir of infamy and inconsideration. He shivered and pulled up the covers around his neck, a move which only revealed his bird dog and his feet. Now he hated his feet, which were white paddles. They were not the honest arched dusky feet of the world's real people. They were the splayed white paddles of the superfluous. He staggered across the hall into the bathroom and sat down. His bowel movement was so shocking it sent his dog scurrying for cover as a blast of discolored water arced from his ass to the crockery. "What lucky girl will get me next?" he moaned aloud. When he made it to the sink and had an opportunity to stand before the mirror, he was not cheered. His face was colorless. His eyelashes seemed to be irregularly spaced. There were greenish-gray shadows in the bottom of every wrinkle and crease. When he pressed down on his teeth, one incisor seemed to send out a little red signal of meaningless pain. A guy ought to bag it, Lucien thought, right here. But who would feed Sadie? Who would rattle the vitamin-enriched kibble into the little sucker's spun-metal bowl? Who would refill her water and run her in her roading harness off-season? Tears filled Lucien's eyes. He knew she needed him, that no one else would remember her points and retrieves. They would take her for a brown and white cur with no master. It would be sadder and more sickening than Old Shep. How would Sadie watch me die? I suppose with a mixture of pride and dismay. At this thought, Lucien laughed miserably. More than anything, he wanted to grow up. But today he was going to do something about it.

Tompkins came down from the corner of Callender. He was wearing a herringbone topcoat with a velvet collar and a John B. Stetson hat. He used his cigarette to point

85

out a streetside stairway to Lucien. They went up and opened the door at the top, going through a very ancient-looking brick wall. Inside was a simple dining room. Adjoined to it by a half door was a small kitchen, where a Chinese woman cooked. "I've got some fine sour-mash whiskey for us, Lucien."

"I don't care how it tastes so long as it kills brain cells and fucks up my memory."

Wick made two strong drinks at a sideboard and silently held the glasses over the half door until the Chinese woman filled them with ice. He brought them to the table and sat down.

"What is this place?"

"This is the dining room. Shitalmighty, I can't eat like those people out there. I don't believe in the afterlife. You have to believe in the afterlife to eat like those sumbitches."

Lucien stared around at the walls of the tall room. It was painted an ocher color and had a ceiling fitted roundabout with hard pine molding. Someone had painted the ceiling a thrilling azure, and plummeting through this blue were all the fine hawks of the northern Rockies, all the common ones, anyway; and from the light fixture which served as a noon sun in this conceit, a terrific prairie falcon hurtled, its feathers scaling its earthward dive with martial brightness.

The Chinese woman came and put down some leek soup, some delicious pot stickers and a bowl of dry fried beef. Most of the light in the room came from the top of the tall transom windows; it was light from a high part of the sky and seemed to filter any life that surrounded the building. In such isolation, Lucien thought, one must decide upon things, accept the aerial quality of one's situation.

"I called my wife."

"She's not your wife anymore."

"I called Suzanne. She seems to have no interest in coming out here. At this time."

"What's there to come to?"

"I know."

"Are you going to do anything about it?" Wick asked in a challenging tone.

"I'm going to start something tremendous," Lucien retorted.

"What?"

"I don't know, but I'll be very proud of it." In Lucien's face was the glow and pride of a diving catch. It was important to snap Wick back just a little. "I'm going to set the world on fire."

"Lucien, it's me, Wick."

"People will come from miles around," he continued, trying to fuel the mood.

Wick stood up and looked upon Lucien with a lowered brow that seemed to say, I know you've got it in you. It was an artificial look. "I have to leave," he said. "Believe this or not, I've got a client. Finish your lunch and don't fuck the cook."

•-•-•-•-•-•-•-•-•-•-•-•-•-•-•-•-•-•-•-•-•-•-•-•-•-•-•-•-•-•-•-•-•-•-•-•-•-•-•-•-•-•-•-•-•-•-•-•-•-•-•

It began to soak in. It soaked in faster than the Chinese food. Lucien headed for the bank, where **9** he was strangely unspecific with a vice-president, who agreed that the ranch was valuable and the loan Lucien wanted would be well secured. Yet when Lucien said, "I just feel lost. I'm hoping heavy borrowing will create a useful crisis," he saw the banker was lost too but unwilling to consider embezzlement or any of the other things that would restore the oxygen to his atmosphere. Even with his blow-dry shag haircut, the banker retained a hangdog face; and nothing on its surface really changed when Lucien said the following. "I know this is all based on you throwing me into the briar patch of usurious interest rates. But I just don't see the thrill from your point of view, however it turns out. Not that I don't appreciate it!" He waved the big check in gratitude and went back outside, where yet another unique sedan suddenly seemed to hold the absolute promise of a rocket ship or a bomb.

Before he started, he wanted to take another good look at the spring. He drove out on a highway interrupted by the tongues of old wheel-packed snow; he went up through his outbuildings, past the house, where Sadie leapt behind the front window. He made his way over the unnerving shalerock jeep road until he reached the spring. He didn't get out. He just sat in the car and listened to the livestock report on the radio and viewed the rolling steam climbing from the great blue eye that had watched him from days gone by. Around the spring, the steam had mineralized the landscape, the branches of trees. Minerals, Lucien knew, were a big item. The spring was a deep penetration of warm moving water as full of goodness as amniotic fluid is to a developing infant. All I've got to do, he thought, the big check burning a hole in his pocket, is deliver the goods. He felt better already, monstrous almost.

They brought the buildings from near and far: a cavalry stable from the Missouri River housed the main pool.

Evocative bentwood dude-ranch furniture from the twenties was arranged around the slate perimeters of the spring, concealing the old mud banks where Lucien had floundered away many a sorrow. Adjoined by a fragrant, carpentered cedar passage was an ancient way station found at Silver Star, Montana; here Lucien's friend and chef Henchcliff prepared the meals that made him a regional legend. Then line shacks from the slopes of Kid Royal Mountain and the high pastures of Froze-to-Death were dismantled, moved and restored as the evocative cottages that housed chiefs of state, high-spirited young professionals, screaming mimis and the assorted preposterously well-off who drifted around the good places on a seasonal basis.

Mary Celeste had set up her enema therapy center in an old-time blacksmith's shop, also connected to the spring; on its walls were loops and loops of glass tubing where the gastrointestinal burden of her clients flew by; she could tell booze from water, beets from a bleeding ulcer and bacterial diarrhea from bad cocaine. She had the mind of a native healer, and no sense of humor.

The landscaping was the original sage and juniper, divided by gravel walks. The parking lot was hidden in a draw and the airfield was on the low flat mesa where, as a boy, Lucien had seen the lost saddle horse with his father.

Old man McCourtney was the doorman, the shell-shocked Irishman with a mottled face. He wore English suits and indicated the front desk with a shaking hand. Since he looked too old and weak to fight, he made a perfect bouncer in the late evenings, preying on the remorse of drunks. Lucien had renewed their friendship at his father's funeral, where he had requested no keening;

McCourtney stood well off among the casual acquain-
tances, twitching. Lucien had had little to say at the
time, as he gripped his mother just above the elbow and
hoped for the best. At the funeral, Lucien said, "If you
ever need me, call." She never called.

Much trouble came to Lucien through his living in an
area his friends wished to visit without their wives. When
Lucien got the hot spring, friendships that had fallen into
rueful desuetude came back to life. They loved him and
they loved his healing waters! They parked on the white
gravel, soaked and appealed for discounts on their bills.
On the radio, a song spoke of one of sixteen vestal virgins
heading for the coast. This is life, thought Lucien, this is
the long tunnel. Down in my hot spring the women are
buoyant with reproductive glee. It draws customers like
flies. Cash discounts for the criminally insane.

Among Lucien's customers were many who bore his
study: a luckless parvenu, girl cowboys, environmental
guides, a geothermal engineer who told Lucien what was
wrong with his hot spring, how it would dry up, etc., a
Hindu, a jockey named "Mincemeat," and so on. There
was a gangster retired to his Madonna collection and
prayer. On Saturday night in the bathrooms next to the
bar, urine's vitreous ring was a carillon of high spirits
from the happy toilets.

Lucien called Suzanne and described his success. This
was going to be a wonderful summer out west.

Then Suzanne called Lucien late one night, so late that
Lucien wondered momentarily where he was. He had
hung a sport coat on the tall bedpost for dry-cleaning the
next day; for a moment he thought the coat had placed
the call to him. His bird dog stood and arched her back

in a slow stretch, not anxious to start the day in the middle of the night.

"What's up?"

"I'm sorry to be calling you so late, but I'm in such a state of confusion I can't sleep."

"Think nothing of it. I've done this to you, often and drunkenly."

Suddenly a silence from Suzanne's end of the line was filled with sobbing. Lucien pulled himself up against the bedstead and waited alertly for her to recover. "What is it?" he asked. "Suzanne, what is it?"

"Lucien, I don't know. I'm going in circles. I'm worn out trying to work and stay ahead of James and I'm just absolutely going in circles. And I miss you. Suddenly you're strong and I'm a mess."

Lucien ached sharply. He missed Suzanne too; but maybe he just missed their old hopes, now long in the past.

"What can I do?" Lucien asked. "I'll do absolutely anything."

"Don't hang up on me."

"I won't hang up on you."

"There. I think I'm better."

"Haven't you met anyone nice yet?"

"Oh, sure. They're everywhere. And you?"

"Well, you know all about the Emily thing," Lucien gasped. "After that I pretty much concentrated on staying fluid, you know. The old moving target trick."

"Target. You're darn lucky you didn't turn into one while she was still there."

"That'll be enough of that, Suzanne. This time I mean it."

"I'm sorry," she said miserably. Lucien turned the

light back off and sat in the dark once again with the silent telephone. They could have been in the same room.

"Why don't you pick up and come out here for a while?"

"I don't know. I've got relatives all over the place there."

"Please."

"You come up with a presentable plan and we'll see."

This was the Suzanne Lucien remembered best. Touching, emotional, sweet and predacious. When she hung up, he lay there used and overjoyed. He could barely get back to sleep. There was moonlight. But when he awakened in the morning he was nervous and didn't want breakfast.

Lucien was doing something very acceptable to everyone: he was making money hand over fist. He wasn't quite certain why this had such a miraculous effect on his self-esteem. After all, the same old battered soul still lived inside the groomed monster Lucien felt he had become. It didn't even arouse his cynicism. I have to admit, he thought, they all like me better now that I am a rich SOB. And some of the hollow feeling had gone, too. It was strange not to be desperate. In fact, he rather missed desperation now that it was gone. It had been an old friend and had produced some top fireworks. Lucien knew, though, that he had been allowed to make mankind's favorite experiment, that of going from some form of rags to some form of riches, overnight. Only he was plagued by the questions: Am I a new man? Why do they like me? Am I secretly the same old shitheel, the same old wino from hell who brought down hurricanes of scorn on himself? Is this an American dream?

He began once again to bring Suzanne and James within reach. He asked if they would come back and got a no. He asked if they would just come up and "give it a try." That didn't work either. Evidently she was serious about presenting a plan. It was only by offering what was in effect a prepaid vacation that he began to get somewhere. "Let's keep it fairly short," said Suzanne. "I don't want to be there with James when Emily returns. She might have an itchy trigger finger."

Lucien gave a warm and appreciative laugh, like the sidekick of a talk-show host. "No, no, no," he said in a rich voice. "I'm afraid we've seen the last of her."

"I'll bet you've got a million more where that one came from," said Suzanne.

To begin with, nothing is merrier than a Rocky Mountain airport in the summertime. Nothing. Lucien stood among the small crowd awaiting passengers and watched the big jet pivot against the shimmering sagebrush flats and come to the ramp. There were numerous people Lucien recognized in the group, and he nodded genially to them like a man of substance, or at least a man not to be lightly disturbed. Perhaps some of these people remembered the old Lucien and took his current stance as an absurdity.

And then the doors opened. People flowed into the airport from the jet. They kept coming, the strangers. And there they were! James in clownish checkerboard shoes, thick glasses and a frightened grin. Next to him walked Suzanne, the same tall brown-eyed girl he'd misunderstood for so long. In her face the contradictions of this arrival were transmuted into wry cheer. She carried a straw bag and moved James along with a hand on the back of his head.

Lucien was head over heels in love. He had never been so in love in his life.

---

Lucien lit a cigarette. He'd almost quit; then the spring was a success and now he chain-smoked like a foundryman. He was back in Wick Tompkins's office, secure in its club-like atmosphere with the reassuring clacking of the computer keyboard coming from the next room.

# 10

"I thank the Savior for taking my tired feet from the long road of loneliness," said Lucien.

"You are full of yourself."

"Well, they're back."

"Anything else you'd care to tell me?"

"Yeah, Wick, I was wondering how come I'm so smart and rich."

Tompkins stared across a pile of uniform green books marked with numerous pieces of folded paper. "It must've been something you ate," he said. "Where's the little family now?"

"I'm letting them sleep."

"And, for example, where are you letting them sleep?"

"I've got them at the White Cottage, the one with the cabana and wading pool."

"Why not with you?"

"The truth is, I'm not sure the Savior actually got me off the long and lonely road at all. Suzanne is viewing this strictly as a vacation. I mean strictly. And my boy looks at me very remotely."

"How long will they be here?"

"Couple of weeks. Maybe more. Y'know, if I pave a glorious trail for their good times. But I can't just phone this one in. I've really got to be on deck. Besides, I'm in love."

"With whom?"

"With Suzanne."

"You're joking."

"No."

"You're shitting me."

"No," said Lucien. "It was love at first sight. Last night at the airport."

"Let me just say this: I approve in a very nonspecific way. Will I be retained as counsel?"

"Yes," said Lucien. "In due course." Lucien was no longer hungry. Though he understood it could never last, he felt himself to be autocratic, satisfied and self-absorbed. For him, that made a nice picture. He got up. "I'm going to go," he said. "It's after ten. They should be up by now."

"As you wish," said Wick. "I have to get in eight billable hours in the next ninety minutes, then go to lunch."

"You're like a brother to me," said Lucien.

"I've come to sense that," said Wick joylessly. "Call me when the roof falls in."

Now Lucien went to see Suzanne and James at the White Cottage. He came through the gate in the wooden wall that gave the place privacy. Suzanne was in a lounge chair reading, her hair tied back exposing the crooked hairline that Lucien had never appreciated but was one of the many things people always found pretty about her. James was knee-deep in the wading pool. "Good morning!" said Suzanne. She lay the book with its spine up in her lap. Lucien went to the pool, where James tossed water back and forth between his hands, nervously watching Lucien. Lucien dropped to one knee and gave James a small embrace.

"Ow," said James. "My sunburn."

Suzanne got up, and for a moment Lucien could still see her shape in the plastic cross-straps of the chaise longue. The book was a traveler's introduction to the Seychelles. Lucien wondered if she had a trip planned there with someone.

"Pop," said James, "want to see me do a racing turn?"

"You bet I do."

James thrashed to the far end of the wading pool, inverted and shot back toward Lucien underwater. When he burst out, there was a sort of brief pride in his face as water streamed down it; and then it was gone.

Suzanne returned to her chaise with a glass of ice water. Lucien sat down a little awkwardly next to her in a kitchen chair, resting his arms on its back. "Maybe we could get someone for James and have dinner together?"

"No," she said.

"Oh, all right. Perhaps another time."

Lucien got no response to this. Instead Suzanne said, "I wonder if tomorrow James and I could borrow a car. I want to get some groceries."

"That's a handy little kitchenette, isn't it?"

"He and I will be eating in."

"Well, sure. You just ring Antoinette, who is my secretary. She'll have someone drive you down."

"I'd really prefer it if we had our own car."

"Easily arranged."

"Thank you."

"James," said Lucien, "am I going to see you later on?"

"Ask Mom," said James nervously. Lucien thought it was time to go. By the time he got out the door, Suzanne was reading her book on the Seychelles again. When he closed the door to the gate, Lucien heard her exclaim, "Goodbye, Lucien! Thanks for everything!" Then in a conversational voice, "I guess he's gone."

He had dinner with Dee instead. Afterward they went to the supper club for dancing and power drinking. An illegal poker game started up and everyone got kicked out by eleven. Lucien drove Dee to her car, parked back of the bank.

"Tonight, sex is out," said Dee.

"I feel the same way," he said, and they parted. He liked her. Dee.

"Stop right there," came the voice, soft, yet clear enough in the tall wooden bedroom where Lucien had slept the long night, the rain impelled horizontally at the panes of glass opposite his pillow. The hot summer lightning cracked into the smoky hayfields that surrounded the old ranch on every side. Lucien looked straight into the rifle barrel first, because it was closest to his head, then followed it back to the sights, the stock, then the face, as expressionless as a blister.

"Are you with one of the churches?"

"No," said the man. "I'm with one of the women. I'm with Dee."

But I was in bed by eleven, thought Lucien. And this time I never laid a hand on her. What is meant by this gun barrel? I imagine we shall see in the next few minutes. Times like these turn the happiest memories into affliction. Even the memory of Dee's bright gaze withered before this weapon.

"Let's get a bite to eat," said Lucien, throwing his feet out onto the cold floor and silently promising himself never to touch a drop again. "My stomach thinks my throat's been cut."

Normally an adroit cook, Lucien felt a cold breeze in his bathrobe as he shakily prepared breakfast, slivering the green chilies into the bowl of eggs, the Black Diamond cheddar, the scallions, the garlic, the microscopic, brutal bird peppers, the sprigs of dill. He reached around the gun to give Gale—that was his name—a smell. Gale nodded, just passing the product through to the skillet: no approval particularly. Gale was bandy with sloped shoulders and flat mosaic knuckles displayed against the wood of the rifle stock. Lucien felt that he would have to say a string of stupid things to get Gale to actually open fire. Gale was starting to get hungry. We must see our way humanely through this: Gale has lost his momentum, is wondering if his manhood is in question.

Lucien put the two plates on the table with glasses of orange juice and a porcelain pot of good coffee. They sat down, Gale with the rifle across his lap. Without emphasis, the gun had become silly. Gale made an attempt at equitability by eating fast: the bird peppers kicked in. Tears burst from Gale's eyes and his face turned blood-red. He set his mouth ajar and stared in terrible thought.

"A touch of the vapors?" Lucien asked.

"—in the fuck you put in these aigs?"

"I'll get you some water."

Lucien hurried. He carried ice water from the refrigerator to the breakfast table, where he threw it in Gale's face and confiscated the gun.

"Gale, stay right where you are for a sec—" Lucien racked open the bolt, ejected the magazine. There were no cartridges in the gun. He handed it back to Gale.

"They say you can set one of these off with your toe," said Gale, morosely gesturing to the rifle.

"Not if it isn't loaded," said Lucien, wondering if this was not slightly at Gale's expense.

"I seen on TV the other day where death is kind of a tunnel," said Gale. Death? "But what few these folks that's come back claim that first mile is hell."

"Let's not talk about death."

"Your house needs a rain gutter," said Gale.

"I don't get it."

"Well, I'm in the seamless gutter business. And I'm about to go broke."

"How much is this going to cost me?"

"I'll make it easy on you. You've got to have it."

"All right, Gale, goddamn it."

On this note Lucien drifted back: Dee is on the balls of her feet, on the seat of the sedan, saying "Ow!"; Lucien administers a spray lubricant associated with outboard motors, getting nowhere. They smell of mosquito dope. A wobbling fly rod indicates galaxies in the summer night sky. She looks fixedly through the rear window. Lucien reads the odometer and wishes every mile could tell a story. A garland of luck to previous owners, and to all those who like blondes with whiskey tenors, collapsed lungs or gas problems, as they are difficult to portray romantically, even to yourself; I didn't know at the time I was buying seamless gutters. Lucien realized he was staring at Gale only when Gale said sharply, "Don't feel sorry for me."

After Gale left, Lucien made a short float on the river, watching rocks become ghosts in the green clarity. The river was consecutive loops of emerald where one could drift for hours and end up a ten-minute walk from the car. A squall stood over the first big bend, hanging within its own envelope of unearthly light. Water streamed from the blades of Lucien's oars white as platinum. The transom of the dory lifted and fell in the choppy water as the river swept him under the thunderhead. Lucien folded the oars so that the boat drifted like a sleeping gull; he tucked his head inside his windbreaker and watched the river sweep him out of the little squall, onto the broads where trout dimpled its silky perfection and aquatic insects soared in the changed temperature. Lucien leaned back into the oars and pulled away from a great white boulder, then into a narrow channel, inches from the speeding willows, the bow of the boat a rifle sight down the eye of the current. He had another mile to float, a mile of stony water that took him almost back to the car. Now he was in a hurry to get to work.

He returned to the house and raced through his shower and ablutions, splashing on that fad of his school years, Canoe after-shave lotion. He selected his tie without the normal fuss: their stripes and colors offered the little aesthetic amusement he had of late. Then the phone rang.

He picked it up just as the caller hung up. He slumped in the chair. He knew it was Suzanne. He would have called her at the White Cottage but he felt awkward about it. Maybe James was calling. Maybe he wanted to go fishing. Maybe his sunburn wasn't bothering him anymore. Then the phone rang again and it was Suzanne. "I just called you," she said. "What've you got on for this evening?"

"Not a thing."

"Well, I borrowed a car from your secretary and stocked up for a few days. What about if I made us a nice pork roast and a cold beet salad?"

"I haven't had it since you last made it. I couldn't be happier."

"Around eight?"

"I'll be there."

When he hung up the phone, Lucien clenched his fists in front of him and shook them up and down, humming through his teeth loudly. Then he rubbed his hands together and clapped them once, hard.

Lucien walked in, self-infused vigor taking shape out of old habit. The sulfuric steam plumes had lost the Dantean fugal quality with the coming of summer and stood out over the buildings and against the high dry blue sky with rare gaiety. It was still early in the morning.

There was a meeting of the Deadrock Ladies' Bridge Club. All bluebeards and George Washington look-alikes. Things were quiet.

But Antoinette, the receptionist, had a weary irritated appearance whose meaning Lucien suspected.

"There was a death in Antelope Suite early this morning," she said. "We couldn't reach you at home. There's some snafu about the arrangements. I'm afraid you'll have to sort this one out."

"Who is it?" Lucien's hair stood on end.

"I got your ex a car," said Antoinette as she flipped through the register.

"Who died?"

"Mr. Kelsey."

"Oh, for Christ's sakes, that's clear to some tank town on Lake Erie."

"I wouldn't know."

"I would," said Lucien. "He was going to have his last drink at the bar with me before signing up for the enema training table. Drank a quart of Finlandia. I know the town well."

Lucien went through the glass doors and into the fetid steam. Certainly Antoinette thinks that I am callused, but if I fall apart, what is to become of this place, and all who depend upon me? Heads looked up from the steam, and arms waved or offered favor-currying salutations, down the wavering poolside that took the press out of his shirts before he'd even started his day. He knew many here were afflicted, if only in their thoughts. Lucien himself was no different. He too was afflicted; lately nothing could have been more trying, more purgatorial, than the activities of his poor old dick. Apart from the obvious, it had begun making two streams during urination, one for the bowl, the other filling his shoe or starting him upon an unwelcome dance; often, too, it saved a final spurt for when it had been returned to his pants: things no hot spring cured. Well, we weren't promised an easy road.

One of the employees, a local youngster whose cowboy boots peeped out from the trousers of his hot-spring uniform, stood outside Antelope Suite in shock. "Never seen one of these before, huh?"

"No, sir."

"They say the first mile's hell."

Lucien walked in, gingerly followed by the youth. Mr. Kelsey was still in bed. An unfinished plate of saltimbocca with some julienned vegetables next to it, a *nouvelle cuisine* flourish.

"How in the hell he get this?" Pointing to the food.

"I'm not sure," the boy stammered. Henchcliff, the chef, had pocketed some change here. Kelsey had fed himself very well and expired before his first enema. Mary Celeste would have canceled him when she saw that saltimbocca going by. Then Lucien would have had her to quiet, another day without the river, without running the dog, without excursions in the saddle, nor tonight's dinner with James and Suzanne.

Lucien leaned over; nothing to confirm here beyond the open pores, the sharkfin lips, the unhearing ears, the full mortality beneath monogrammed hot-spring sheets. Kelsey had planned a hair-dyeing experiment. At all events, we must get these leftovers to the shores of Lake Erie, to the shadow of abandoned steel towns, to the windrowed fish and bird bodies of that storied Midwest.

"We're going to need a shipping bag and the air-conditioned station wagon. Make sure Antoinette has contacted next of kin. Have housekeeping stand by. I'll be in my office."

Lucien walked the long corridor. He rang Antoinette. "Antoinette, *re* Kelsey: A. Get him embalmed. B. Get him a container. C. Ship him home. And when you confirm shipment with next of kin, verify the new billing address." Lucien hung up and sighed. He buzzed again. "Make sure Mary Celeste is not still awaiting Mr. Kelsey. Then come in here for a letter."

Antoinette appeared in about five minutes with a spiral notebook and pen. The last ten percent of her looks were still there to extrapolate the loss from. "This one is to the Chamber, attention of Donald Deems. 'Dear Donald, Do you think it is right that I should be asked to offer a rate reduction for the sister-city delegation when, one, no one knows the size of that delegation, and two, no one else in town is making a similar contribution to the success of the show? See you Thursday. Write it down. All best, Lucien.' " He looked up at Antoinette. "Chop chop. Today's mail."

Lucien hated having to be this way with Antoinette. But in the first six months of work she'd gone on and on about her no-good husband, her car loan and her period. Then she left her husband, and every time she had a new boyfriend there was a renewed outbreak of cystitis and she'd whine on about the cost of antibiotics, conspiracies between the AMA and pharmaceutical manufacturers to keep the prices up, and so on. Endless bladder-infection chats had finally turned Lucien into a man who watched his topics.

When she was gone, Lucien sighed, "A cowboy's work is never done," and started through his papers. Lang and Hughes in New York had sent the new ads, and they reflected the greater specificity he had requested: "Sun 'n' Sulfur" for the travel magazines, "Minerals Plain" for *The New Yorker* with a wide-angle of the sage barrens making them look like a grass court. He vetoed for the last time, he hoped, an overweight children's wing because of the inchoate evil he felt in the presence of fat youngsters. The very young failed to see the point of a rich mineral spring; they ran around yelling Who Cut the Cheese and other zircons of new wit. Besides that, a day that began with the purchase of seamless gutters to keep from provoking a scandal left a lot to be desired.

He went through the back of the kitchen, where a refrigerator truck of fresh fruit and vegetables from Oregon was being unloaded. "Hello, Henchcliff," he called out. "How is it by now?" Henchcliff, whose habit it was to dress on or off the job like a prison trusty, twisted his head quickly in the don't-ask-me of the perpetually angry. But Henchcliff had the touch. He was under the brutal constraint of cooking only longevity food, like so many of the nutritionists who made the rounds of spa kitchens. Henchcliff could loosen up, pour on the cholesterol, salt and grease with the best of them. On his best behavior, however, he sent forth hundreds of dewy, steamy, identical, fructoid marvels through the double doors to the fruit bats around the spring. How they could eat in the steam was beyond Lucien; but he was entrepreneur enough to recognize that dining on row crops half invisible to one another in an ambience that anywhere else would have gagged them was part of the mystique, part of what they took home to their dense-pack satellite homes, in gratitude. Pink faces hung mysteriously over the greenery in the steam. *Satisfied* faces, thought Lucien.

The candy kitchen occupied the west side of the main cooking area: it always surprised Lucien they could sell as much of the sulfur taffy as they did. But month after month it was a list leader, solid as a good franchise. Most people kind of choked them down like medicine, despite that no one claimed they were anything but candy. They did smell just like the spring, though, and nostalgia crops up in the least expected places.

He went out the far door and knocked at Dominic's room. This used to be a bed-sitting room for the chef. It was no longer needed, now that Henchcliff lived in town.

It was isolated from the rest of the compound and made Lucien a little more comfortable. Dominic had many grave enemies, and it was good to have him in a less populated spot in the event of a rubout. Dominic was their only permanent guest.

Dominic called for him to enter in his pure, strange soprano. Lucien thrust half his body in. "Just saying hi."

Dominic held up a Madonna made of blue smoked glass. "A new one," he said. "From Sainte Anne de Beaupré in Quebec." He set it on the shelf with the others. "Go on. I see y'busy."

Back at reception and a quick fan through the receipts. He looked up to see the station wagon cruise past on the pea rock toward the back of the building. Should have been gone by now.

"Got ahold of the next of kin?"

"No problem," said Antoinette.

"Billing?"

"American Express. They had duplicate cards."

"What about the autopsy?"

"They're going to pass. They wanted him hermetically sealed rather than embalmed. The state requires one or the other. He's in the container now."

Lucien gazed irritatedly out to the empty parking area. "Tell Zane to get a move on," he said. "It looks hot out there. I'm going to work in the office. No calls." Lucien headed back off down the corridor.

Antoinette yelled out: "Someone phoned about seamless gutters. Said the price had gone up."

"Oh, for Christ's sakes."

Lucien sealed himself in the office. Quick look at his watch: two hours' light to ride home and run the dog, then dinner with Suzanne and James.

He called for current balances in the springs account, the ranch account, his personal account and wrote them into the respective books. Deadrock Plumbing. This bill can't be real. No real bill can be this size. These drifters need a moving target.

"Tim Lake. This is Lucien Taylor." After a little bit: "Tim, you send me this bill?"

"Yes, Lucien, I did."

"Tim, you've got the balls of a brass monkey."

"Lucien, you're lookin' at a lot of hours on that sheet. I had three men up there, two trucks."

"I've seen that before. One truck is to make beer runs when your rummies get the DTs working on my furnace. Tim, I'm gonna give you a break. I'm gonna rip this goddamned sonofabitch up and not let you hurt my feelings. You go sit down and write me a bill you take some pride in. But this time be honest. With yourself."

Then, while the glow was upon him, though the age of bowmen and harpers was lost for all time, he could dash off some price-control letters. He rang Antoinette. Gone home. The phone was done for the day. He felt the earth move. Lucien pulled off his tie, examining its red and silver silk stripes for the first time, rolled it and put it in his pocket. He wandered down the corridor, seeing with satisfaction the cowboy and cowgirl waiters moving in the steam. Mary Celeste table-hopped with nutritional tips in a drooping dinner gown; her Empire coif listed very slightly to the north. In a couple of hours all but the minimum lights would have been turned off; most guests would be in their quarters. A few with wooing twinkles would be back in the main pool, paddling through stench to desire. There's a little of that in all of us.

There was time to take a shower and shave once again,

inspecting his face for missed spots. Then he put on some invigorating lotion and watched himself button a blue-and-white-striped shirt. He had slicked his hair straight back like a rich heir, and he withdrew his lips so he could pass judgment on his teeth: bright gums, no plaque; the crown doesn't appear unless one smiles too hard, as in drunkenness or, once a year, delight. He walked to the White Cottage, a bright and romantic rental unit in the wind-trained junipers above the spring. It did well.

He knocked at the gate. Suzanne opened the door for him and returned immediately to the small compound. Where the sliding doors opened on the wading pool, James sat reading comic books. He probably does that a lot, Lucien thought. When he'd last seen James he really wasn't interested in comics. He still had an extensive GI Joe collection. Now he wore camouflage and read comics.

"Can I make you a drink?"

"Are you having one?"

"I'm having quite a few," she said.

"Okay," Lucien said. "The usual."

"I don't know what the usual is," said Suzanne, making one slow blink.

"It's anything but scotch," said Lucien. "Like how about some bourbon and water?"

"I'm not sure we have it."

"What's this tone?"

"No tone. I just didn't know if it was there."

Lucien sat next to James.

"Hi, Pop."

"Well, what do you think?"

"Are you making a fortune?"

"I'm doing okay."

"I wish we could make a fortune. Me and my mom. Maybe I'll invent something."

Suzanne returned with the drinks and sat in a wicker chair opposite Lucien and James. "Dinner failed," she said with an inquisitive smile, as if to say, Now what?

"It can't have. You made that pork roast a hundred times."

"Goes to show you about memory," she said.

"Do you want me to ring over to the kitchen?" Lucien asked evenly.

"I made something else. I was going with a terrific cook. He showed me a way to do calves' liver. Yes and you're going to love it."

"He was a cook?"

"He was an investment analyst and a college vice-president, but he liked to cook, Lucien. He liked to cook."

"I'll bet that's not all he liked to do."

She pulled her pearls out from the collar of her blouse, regarded James with a smile and said, "Come to dinner."

Instead of place mats, Suzanne had used parts of that night's newspaper. Lucien had railroad cutbacks. James had sports. Lucien couldn't see what Suzanne had. Their plates were stacked like the silverware, to be passed around. The dinner was in one deep skillet with a serving spoon. Suzanne used to make a great effort at presentation. When Lucien tasted his food, he found her cooking had improved considerably. There was some jug red wine and water glasses.

"How was your day?"

"Amazingly complicated," said Lucien.

"We rather thought you'd come by," said Suzanne.

"One of my guests died," Lucien boomed over the liver. "I had to arrange shipment."

There was quiet as James stared with youthful ghoulishness. He cut his eyes to his mother in hopes of a deeper inquiry about the man who died. Then the three went on eating. Lucien couldn't believe James would eat this meal. He'd probably learned to eat what he was given. In Honduras they used to take a table right onto the beach and sink the legs in the sand. They'd throw leftovers profligately to the seagulls and put the juice of wild limes on the mangoes they loved for dessert. They had the shade of the beach plum, and Suzanne would take the trouble of using real linens. Therefore this utilitarian presentation was something of a shock to Lucien. Maybe it was high-tech.

Suzanne got up and left the room. Lucien looked over at James while James ate. It seemed to Lucien that James took extraordinary care in cutting his food into uniform pieces. For a moment Lucien couldn't understand why he did this; then he saw that it was fear that made James so careful.

"We've got to think of something," said Lucien more ingenuously than he usually was with children. "Something we could do for fun."

"What do you want to do?" James asked. He looked ready for flight.

"Do you still like to fish?"

"I haven't done it in a long time."

"What do you do for fun?"

"I fly radio-controlled airplanes."

"Radio-controlled airplanes! What fun is that?"

James was frozen silent. He pushed his jet-black hair sideways as if trying to remember where it was parted. "Anyway, that's what I do," he said in a small voice.

"I just don't know what that is," said Lucien. Then, to makes things better, he asked, "Do you think it's something I'd like?"

"No."

"Jamesie, let's go fishing. Let's try it. If we don't have fun, we'll just quit right then. We'll stop right there and that'll be it. We'll try this radio-control stuff."

"I don't have my plane," said James in terror. "It's not here."

"What's happened to your mother? Go check and see what your mother is up to."

James got up with an air of diffidence and of duty and went into the adjoining rooms. When he returned, he said, "She's not coming out."

"I beg your pardon."

"She said she was sorry."

"Well, I'm sorry too," said Lucien, concealing his shock. "But tomorrow, let's fish or something, okay? And uh, that'll be good, okay? So, around eight o'clock, Jamesie. And you be ready."

Lucien got up and left the White Cottage. He was stunned.

Lucien smoked for a while on the hillside and watched the moon rise, then continued his walk toward the spring. He had learned to gauge the day-use traffic and the activities of the bar merely by the sounds the building itself gave off. It was busy tonight and that was sufficient, though he felt quite sunk. He went alongside the main building, absentmindedly testing the height of the shrubbery plantings with his hand as he went. He could smell curing paint from the new siding, and the deep breath of the

spring was everywhere. A high, hysterical laugh pene-
trated from the bar; then it was quiet again. Lucien
wandered clear around the front of the building to the
parking lot. It was nearly full, many local license plates;
and among the cars was the station wagon.

Lucien walked to the rear window and looked in. *No.*
Though all you could see was the shipping container,
there was Kelsey. Lucien thought, Why have you sent
me this? I'm serious.

He called Antoinette at home. *"Where's Zane?"*

Quiet, then: "Why?"

"Kelsey's still in the driveway."

"Has he missed his plane?"

"Yes, he missed it. It was the Frontier five-fifteen to
Minneapolis."

"I guess Zane got scared."

"Isn't Zane your nephew?"

"Yes . . ."

"I'm in the mood to plow the little shit *way* back."

"I'm sorry, Mr. Taylor."

"The next time you ring in some kinsman, make sure
he's grown fingerprints. Now look, I'm going to haul
Kelsey to the airport. When I get there I'll call you with
his schedule. Then the rest is yours and Zane's."

"I'll take care of it. Do you want to give Zane a second
chance?"

"Not at all."

Huge birds of prey soared in the vague artificial light
over the spring as in a very ancient time; the steam
plumes reached to the birds and didn't quite make it,
though they showed wind shifts sooner than the birds
did. I wonder if they know I've got Kelsey. Lucien started
the engine and drove down to the stables. He yelled in to

Roy to go ahead and feed Lucifer; he had to go to the airport with a guest. What did I do to deserve this?

He stopped in at the Deadrock Bar and Grill for a quick one, and had more than one. The back bar seemed as reassuring as a four-poster on a winter's night. There was a playoff game on the hanging TV and Lucien shouted, "Hook 'em, Horns," until someone next to him reminded him that Texas wasn't in the game. It was Purdue and Somebody State. Nevertheless, there was a lot of handshaking. Here and there an enemy squinting with regal glee. Lucien set his empty drink down hard on the bar to indicate the end. Out with the wallet. "I've got to get my rear end to the airport." The bartender turned to the register.

"The airport is closed."

"*What?*"

The bartender made change blankly and Lucien left it as a tip. He tottered to the door, then swung abruptly to the pay phone. He called Antoinette and explained everything.

"I think you better get some sleep," said Lucien with boozy, inappropriate affection.

"Mrs. Kelsey must be simply shattered beyond words. She's already met one plane," said Antoinette.

"She'll be fine. Call her right now and find out what she wants us to do. Tell her the weather prevented us from getting to the airport today."

Lucien went down the street and watched the teenage girls for fifteen minutes by the clock. Then he returned to the phone. Lucien had decided to lie. Antoinette picked it up.

"Mrs. Kelsey said bury him here. She said she's sick of all this. She says she's had it up to here."

113

"Religious preference?"

"Nondenominational."

"Can we use Dominic's priest?"

Sacajawea Memorial Cemetery had been unsuccessful. Vault rentals were meant to carry the note, but locally it was viewed as citified, a meaningless luxury. Doing this at night took the curse off a death at the spa; so Lucien's crew—his horseshoer Garby, Henchcliff the chef, the ever-considerate Dominic Armada, two waiters Sunshine and Farther, the trail boss Steven Thomas Castine, and Father Alerion—all stood around the viewless dynamite hole at the rear of Sacajawea Memorial, gone Chapter Eleven for its venturesome owner. One little roll and Kelsey seemed to leap into the next world, or at the minimum, the ergonomics of the grave. The staff immediately finished the job with garden tools from the hot spring.

"Our Father—" began Father Alerion, pulling down his Navy watch cap.

"Nondenominational," Lucien reminded him. Alerion sent up weary eyes at him.

"Dear God in heaven—"

"Nope." Lucien shook his head intransigently.

"How 'bout 'Good luck'!" shouted Father Alerion.

So "Good luck" it was, and then a long spell as the earth reclaimed Mr. Kelsey, as the soil of the American West fell upon him; and suddenly, for all of them, there was something sad about this because, for example, who was he? The eight men stood in pyramidical silence.

And now it was very dark, yes, very solemn. Lucien suggested they go back for a small dinner, something, a note in a bottle, from eight strangers, to show that the immemorial balm of mourning was not something absolutely lost to mankind.

"Jesus Fucking Christ," said Henchcliff. "I've been cooking since six this morning."

"I noted some perfect breasts of mallards I shot, enough endive for a big salad, or you are at liberty to braise it. Those lovely new potatoes didn't go unnoticed. Stir-fry the cauliflower as of yore. And I'd like a nice cigar in a number four ring size with a maduro wrapper."

They sat at the long table in the kitchen while an exhausted Henchcliff slammed serving bowls with one hand and reeled around with an expensive cabernet in the other like some anomalous sailor with a family vineyard in Bordeaux. Dominic got tired of this noise and gave Henchcliff his homicidal grin with the veins of his skull in bas-relief: "Y'makin too much noise. Y'folla me?" Henchcliff quieted right down but resorted to breathing through his teeth. One cut of Dominic's rheumy killer eyes and Henchcliff brought that to a stop as well. From Lucien's point of view, Henchcliff was greatly improved.

One of the waiters noted that death was a long tunnel aimed at a cheerful light. Lucien wondered if he had missed a television special. The food was wonderfully prepared, a genuine salute to the departed. Henchcliff sat down, slack with alcohol and the sense he was being used. Dominic gave a very strict recount of the afterlife: heaven, purgatory and hell. Hell was particularly vivid, having been modeled in all its details on New Jersey waste-disposal sites. Purgatory you could hack; and you entered heaven without having to use the stairs, or having to listen to the neighbors screech, and without having to climb over a wino on the front stoop. In heaven you never ran out of silk, patent leather and mohair.

"How about you, Father Alerion?" Lucien asked.

"It's in the Book," said Alerion. "I didn't imagine a word or two on Our Lord's behalf would do any harm."

"I was under strict orders."

"From an apostate?"

"Nope." Lucien speared a slice of rare duck. "His wife." He turned to one hippie waiter. "Clean your plate."

"I have, thanks."

"Attaboy. Now run get Lucifer and bring him to the hitching rack with the plantation saddle. His is the cavalry bridle. 'US' on the cheekbuttons." The waiter got up, a little put out at being removed from the company. "No charge for the meal," Lucien said as the hippie left the room. "Henchcliff, it amazes me how well you cook even when you're in a bad mood. I salute your carry-on-regardless approach to your craft."

"Thank you."

Garby, the horseshoer, grinned through everything with a fixed grateful expression. Lucien thought that if one had nothing to say, it was a successful stance. Experience had shown him, though, that people like this are quick to blow up, and to pummel people around them.

Then it was quiet. It was the middle of the night. Lucien was still toying with the idea, quite genuinely, that Kelsey might as well have been him. When my time comes, I want some ceremony. This was just terrible.

Lucien said goodnight and went out from the front of the main lodge, where Lucifer stood almost imperceptible in the darkness. He threw the reins up over the horse's neck, mounted and rode off.

He took the long way home. His cigar made a ruby light that arced as he held it away from his body and tapped the ash. Suzanne and James would be curled up now. The reins hung in Lucien's fingers like a small plumb weight. Every now and then a bright spark flew from a steel horseshoe and it seemed wonderful how bright and emotionless country air could be. Was Suzanne afraid of him?

Lucien put his horse away and got into bed, into clean sheets and a wool blanket taut across his body. He lay on his back and crossed his arms on his chest. As he drifted into sleep, he pretended he was slipping away from the dock into the next life.

## 13

Lucien got up at daybreak. When he went outside, the moisture was still in the ground and the ground itself seemed to be beginning a day-long respiration as the smell of grass and open dirt and evergreens hung on the unmoving air. He walked down to the corral and opened the gate to the upper pasture. The horses crowded each other in the passage, then ran and bucked onto the new ground. There were flatiron clouds over the far ranges, and they were the color of wet slate. Lucien put his cup of coffee on top of a post and threw some hay up into the metal feeder. He reached through with his jackknife and cut the binder twine, pulled the strings out, looped them and hung them on a plank. The salt was all cupped out from the working of tongues, but more than half the block was left. He could hear the whine of a cold-starting tractor down at the neighbor's ranch. He'll do that until the battery is dead, thought Lucien, then go in and watch the soaps. An old-timer.

He went back up to the house and got a few things. He had a notion. He got a camouflage net and some welder's gloves. He got the little box of bird bands and some pliers, and the long-handled net. He got his wire pigeon cage out of the basement and two pairs of goggles that were hanging on a nail next to the airyway window. He ignored the phone and turned off the low flame under the coffeepot. On the wall was a picture of his father being presented with a spit of roasted meat in a restaurant in Arequipa, Peru. The phone rang again and Lucien did not pick it up. He had come to know when the calls were not urgent, just as he could count heads at the hot spring right through the wall.

He got everything loaded into the car and went over to the White Cottage. He knew it was early. He knew Suzanne would be wandering around in her robe trying to wake up, keeping sleepy responsible eyes on the waking day. As he reached the door in the gate, a cloud of warblers lifted out of the yellow-flowered caragana. He could hear James singing, and when he knocked on the door the singing stopped. "It's Pop!" Lucien called into the quiet. The gate opened and there was Suzanne. Lucien was happy to see her. She smiled with faint embarrassment and murmured something about not coming through at dinner. "Not to worry," said Lucien. "There'll be another time." There was a plate of pastries on the outdoor table, and a pitcher of juice. Lucien recognized every pattern and whorl of the pastry: Suzanne had learned to get what she needed from the kitchen. He took a couple of sweet rolls.

James came out of the cottage, quickly waved, then

turned to look at his mother. "Can't you say good morning to Pop?" she said.

"Good morning."

Lucien ate a sweet roll and watched him for a moment.
That made James nervous. "James, I'm going to band
some hawks today. I want you to help me. We're trying
to figure what all we've got on this place. It's pretty
exciting."

"Weren't we going into town today?" James asked his
mother.

"We can go anytime," she said, trying to messenger
some reassurance James's way with a bright smile.

"But I need gym socks," James said in a panicky voice.
"Remember?"

"I can pick those up."

"Last time they didn't fit," he said in a desperate
whisper.

"You go band hawks with Pop," she said firmly. "I've
got to get dressed." She went back up to the house, hiking
the terrycloth robe around her angular hips. Lucien and
James were alone. Lucien quickly made to open the door.

"Do I need a coat?"

"You're fine. Let's go."

They went out through the gate to the car with the
net-handle sticking out of the back window. "We didn't
bring enough socks," James explained. "And I only got
these one pair of glasses. Me and Mom didn't plan so
good, I don't think."

"Anything you need, you tell me," said Lucien. James
was embarrassed.

By the time they had wound out past the buildings and
started across the ranch, James had his small face angled
unmovingly at the side window of the car. Lucien didn't

know what to do. "James, have I said something wrong?" The land here was flat and brushy and there was an absolutely horizontal butte a few miles ahead.

"No."

"Are you sure?"

"Yes."

Lucien thought for a long, hard moment. "Then why are you treating me like this?"

"Because you're never going to let me go," James said bitterly. "You're going to keep me and never let me go." He began to cry, silently heaving in the huge space of his seat. Lucien shook his head as if to say that weren't true, but he didn't actually say anything. He just kept on driving until James finally sighed.

By that time they reached the old homestead, and Lucien stopped and got out. "Reach me the net, James. We've got to get us a pigeon for bait."

The two of them carried the net into the old barn and were momentarily blinded by the sudden near darkness. Immediately a number of pigeons went out the old haymow; the remainder cycled back and forth overhead, making a hollow, woody racket in the closed space. Lucien gave James the net and the little boy walked around swiping and missing pigeons. Soon he was running after them, and in a minute he brought his net down with the thrashing lump of a pigeon tangled in its mesh. As they put the pigeon into the wire carrying cage, the others assembled cooing on the whitened log joists. Lucien praised him and they took everything back out to the car.

Lucien drove on the zigzag dirt road toward the butte. James carried the cage in his lap and stared in at the now apparently tame pigeon that walked red-eyed back and forth on the wooden floor cooing in an inquiring and flutey voice. "I wonder what that bird is thinking about!" said James.

The road came up under the butte, so close that the rock wall was just outside the window of the car. They drove around to where the end of the butte melted back into the surrounding hills and drove partway out onto the butte itself and stopped. Here the wind had a warm westerly sweep from the valley floor, and they could see the small dust devils from a great distance. The cars on the river road didn't seem to be moving at all.

"I can see some hawks now," said Lucien. "They're in the thermals."

"What's thermals?"

"Warm rising air. Easy for the hawks to fly in. You get the pigeon. I'll get the camouflage net and the rest of it."

Lucien watched James trying to carry the pigeon's cage and look into its side at the same time and thought, as the little boy stumbled along, I can see a beginning.

They carried the gear a half mile out onto the warm top of the butte. Lucien watched James until the boy began to see the hawks. Sometimes the heated gusts would come through the deep grass in cat's paws and they would have to lean into the wind as they walked. Suddenly James looked straight at Lucien and grinned, put down the cage and said, "Gotta rest up."

"I shot a big pronghorn out here when I was a kid," said Lucien.

"With your dad?"

"Nope. By myself. Then I couldn't haul it home. An old cowboy came along with a dog and a pair of binoculars looking for his cattle and we packed it on his horse and we walked out together even though he had real bad knees, real bad. I always thought that was something special. I told the kids at school it was my dad that packed it out, but actually it was this old cowboy and I didn't really even get his name. We gave his dog some antelope. When I was bigger I had some horses of my own, just crow bait—"

"What's 'crow bait'?"

"Used up. I lived with my mother and we didn't have money, not much of it anyway. But even with those old horses, I could go. I could go clear over the top. I could go anywhere." Why am I rambling on like this, Lucien wondered.

James looked all over the top of the butte. "How did we end up in the State Department?"

"I don't know. College. I used to make pictures of all this stuff. I got sick of pictures of this butte. But I never got sick of the butte. I came up here a while ago when there'd been a chinook and there were these wild old patches of snow and I came that close to making one more picture of the place. But I felt like I'd covered that. I just wonder if you have a clue about what I'm saying." James was smiling nervously, one lens of his glasses glinting shut, trying so to please.

They kept on until they came to an oval of rocks on the flattened ground. "I'm ninety-nine percent certain that this is where the Indians caught their birds." Lucien like so many had always felt the great echoes from the terminated history of the Indians—foot, dog and horse Indians. How could a country produce orators for thousands of years, then a hundred years of yep and nope? It didn't make sense. It didn't make sense that the glory days of

122

the Old South were forever mourned while this went unmentioned. Maybe the yeps and nopes represented shell-shock, a land forever strange, strange as it was today to a man and a boy with a caged bird and makeshift camouflage. Well, thought Lucien, it's not a bad spot for coyotes, schemers and venture capitalists.

Lucien laid out the trap carefully. He put on the heavy gauntlets, and they each put on their goggles. He removed the pigeon from the carrying cage and seized its feet in his fingers. The wings beat hard and scared James. The two of them got under the camouflage and Lucien held the bird outside the netting atop their reclined bodies.

The camouflage consisted of numerous yellow and olive strips sewn to a piece of netting. From underneath it, the wind seemed diminished and the sky behind the mesh harsh and clear, vast as a cathedral. The longer they stayed under the net, the more it seemed to curve high over them, as though its sides were somehow not far away and its center absolutely vertical overhead.

"What's going to happen?"

"We hope a hawk will come to us."

"Then what?"

"Then we'll see what he is and we'll put one of those bands on his leg and turn him loose."

"Why's a hawk going to come to us?"

"He's going to try to get our pigeon." The pigeon was murmuring faintly. It had shortened its neck and flared its feathers in peace. Lucien could feel that the clenching of its feet in his hands had stopped. He could sense the heat of the pigeon's body on his own chest and thought he could let go of it without losing the bird.

"I think he's sleepy," said James.

123

"Don't you get sleepy."

"I won't."

Time passed slowly. Lucien's arm was cramping and James was quietly knocking the sides of his tennis shoes together. Then James fell asleep. So Lucien, not concerned about their talk, was able to drift off in a fashion himself. Oddly, he thought about Dee; she'd been with him when he thought he was going to crack, or maybe had cracked. He wondered if she could really be as brutal a floozy as she seemed, always clambering onto all fours to receive her sacrament stern-on. Wonderful how that kind of cartooning took the heat off, made time fly. When he was young he used to shadowbox for the same reason, dancing around, throwing punches, going fifteen rounds in his own world. Then came drinking. Then came Emily and the Lost Sweetheart and the spring, the Lost Sweetheart Spring. Why couldn't he stand success? Suzanne was success. Suzanne was whole. Why was he just beginning to see that?

The pigeon moved. Lucien remained still but noted his head was erect once more, his limpid eyes unmoving. Lucien looked on up to the sky. There was the hawk. The falconers called it waiting-on: the hawk made no motion in the circle of sky but hovered with a blurred wing-beat straight overhead, taking the pigeon's position. The pigeon felt this happening to him. Lucien knew that if he nudged James it would spook the hawk and they'd lose him. Instead he regulated his own breathing and watched until the distant wing-beat stopped, the hawk tightened its size and fell.

When the impact came, James jumped up screaming and began to crawl off. Lucien sat up, holding the hawk by the feet in one gauntleted hand. There were feathers everywhere, and the hawk beat in a blur of cold fury, striking at Lucien with his downcurving knife of a beak and superimposing his own screech over the noise of James. "We've got him, James!" James, quiet now, looked ready to run. The hawk had stopped all motion but kept his beak marginally parted so that the small, hard black tongue could be seen advancing and retreating slightly within his mouth. "It's a prairie falcon. It's the most beautiful bird in the world. I want to come back as a prairie falcon."

"Where are you going?"

"Nowhere very soon. Reach me a band and the pliers." James handed these things to him gingerly. It fascinated Lucien that he was such a timid boy. Lucien hadn't been particularly timid and he rather liked having a boy who was. But James was shaking.

Each time the bird's wings beat, Lucien could actually feel the lift in his forearm, could feel the actual pull of the falcon's world in the sky. He had seen hawks on the ground, graceless as extremely aged people, and he knew their world was sky. He'd seen old cowboys limp to their horses, then fly over the land, and he knew what their world was too. He wanted his own life to be as plain.

By concentration and by ignoring the prospects of a bite, Lucien managed to get the band on. "We're married at last," he said to the hawk. James raised his eyebrows. Lucien held the terrifying bird out before him and released his grip. The falcon pulled vertically from his glove and with hard wing-beats made straight into deep sky, swept straight off and was gone.

When Lucien looked over at James, he was holding the pigeon in his hands. Its eyes were closed. Its head was angled harshly onto its back. Blood ran from the nostrils down the domestic blue feathers of its narrow shoulders. Lucien said nothing.

"We both fell asleep at the same time," said James in an unsteady voice.

---

Today was not going to be a day to be scattered and worried. Today he would indulge a few small preferences like **14** keeping the house temperature low and wearing a sweater. He would read Lord Byron's letters. Evidence indicates that alcohol's irritating effects on Byron's urogenital tract forced him to seek relief in blind liaisons of the sex type, producing children, which Byron called hostages to oblivion. He got that one right. From a burning sensation to a dynasty in three steps. Byron and his poor old dick.

He boiled two eggs. He had a porcelain eggcup that he'd had for thirty years. He had a set of silver military brushes given to him as a baby. He had his first fishing license from back in the days when you could buy worms along the road and get angling tips from the barber. A bit of moving water then was an exaltation of riches; the eggcup and the military brushes connected him to a time he intended to return to. And with each passing year he failed more miserably. As he sliced the tops of the eggs off and checked their doneness with the curve of spoon, he thought, Perhaps a little country with slaves in it would be better, for my very own. His mind drifted away to possible chancelleries, the Archbishop's study connected by tunnel to the back of his fireplace, a thundering speedboat to move over territorial tidewaters with President Lucien at the helm, *cher*, all alertness for counterrevolutionary elements attempting a landing. That's what the eggcup did to him, took him back to when all was possible.

Then the phone rang.

"Where did you put Kelsey?"

"Well, we finally got him out of the station wagon," Lucien laughed. "Who's this?"

"This is his wife."

"Oh, God, are you serious?"

"I am indeed. Your secretary gave me your number after I'd threatened her good."

"Well, we buried him, actually, uh, ma'am. At Valleyview. Here in Deadrock."

"Valleyview."

"Yes, ma'am."

"Sounds real Kodachrome. I'll tell you what we need up here estatewise, is about six copies of the death certificate. You handle that?"

"I can."

"Your people got the address here; I just received Kelsey's bill."

"Yes, ma'am."

"It's pure-D exorbitant. What in God's name were you feeding him?"

"We—"

"Anyway, he isn't missing anything. I'll wait on the certificates. Thanks for your efforts. G'bye."

Lucien hung up. If that doesn't do it, what will? He knew he had gotten ahead of himself when he buried Kelsey.

Lucien went through the front door of the hot spring and into the front office. Antoinette sat on the corner of the reception desk. She was waiting for him.

"Dig him up," said Lucien

"What?"

"We have to dig up Kelsey."

"I don't believe this," said Antoinette.

"We don't have a death certificate. We can't get one without the coroner's report."

Lucien had been through his share of burials, certainly ones closer to him than this. But having to dig up Kelsey made all the others seem not final. It wouldn't do. It would make things seem like some medieval uproar with loosed spirits ranging about among live people.

"He had a twinkle in his eye, that Kelsey." Antoinette said this with the innocence of an aborigine sticking something into another mammal and breaking it off.

"You're on the detail to dig him up," said Lucien simply. It was the acme of infantilism.

At the cemetery a big yellow backhoe was off to one side, and a stranger in coveralls was viewing the bag containing Kelsey. Antoinette sobbed uncontrollably in her camel's-hair coat and cowboy boots. Two pool cleaners were coming to load Kelsey to the coroner's office. "Call Mrs. Kelsey once he's delivered. Tell her he's all hers. I hope it's the last I hear of him in this life." Lucien cut his eyes to the container. "What a thing to say about a companionable fellow like that." He returned the questioning stare of the man in coveralls. "So many of our customers are people you hate like heck to spend an evening with. This guy had one good story after another."

Lucien paused by his car and, without turning to face Antoinette, urged her to get a grip on herself. Beyond the low line of foothills he could hear the iron connecting of trains. The low drifting smoke from the plywood mill came ghostly through the coulees as thermals changed in the approaching afternoon. Overhead two groups of crows passed each other, one going to the river, the other to the hills. Imagine if the papers got a picture of those boys sitting on Kelsey. Remains of area industrialist handed over to carrion birds in Montana. Are we one nation or not. The civil war where you least expect it.

Lucien stood by the galvanized tank and ran water for his horses, the hose three feet under and sending up circling shafts of yellow straw through the dark water to show it in motion. Over the white pipe fence the cedars twisted in the wind. Lucien thought, What am I looking for? What in the world?

Where hard spring snow had turned enamel under the huge pines, sudden birds' shadows now appeared, then went; Lucien carried buckets of grain and thought, It has lasted until June, a miracle which may have fallen on Thanksgiving. His spirits were starting up. They would stay up for a while if they could get Kelsey buried once and for all.

As Lucien thought about it, he really didn't know what the effect of trapping the hawk had been on James, what kind of day it had made. When Lucien had dropped him off, the White Cottage was full of Suzanne's relatives, mostly cousins and including a good number of no-accounts who had nothing better to do than give Lucien a dirty look as one who'd done a good girl wrong. There was a cousin from Great Falls who used to run a greasy spoon up that way that was open twenty-four hours a day and therefore had no doorknobs. On days he wanted to fish and could find no one to spell him, he wrapped a hundred feet of logging chain around the building and padlocked it. He alone smiled at Lucien standing awkwardly in the doorway, the unwelcome host. But early Tuesday morning Suzanne called and said that James had enjoyed his day.

"Did he say anything about the pigeon?"

"Yes."

"Did that upset him?"

"He seems to appreciate that you and he had some kind of adventure. When I said it was sad about the pigeon, he said that's how hawks have to live. He was kind of taking up for you in that, I thought."

"That's nice."

"So things aren't as bleak as you may believe."

"It serves my purposes to feel that I am singled out. I get mad. Which serves to get me out of bed in the morning."

"Do you remember my cousin Danny?"

"Not really."

"Well, he wants to know if you can use an irrigator."

"I want to hold you and kiss you."

"You stop this right now."

"We don't need an irrigator. We put in a wheel-line sprinkler and we don't use it. We just write it off. Lying there, it underscores the nothing-is-real atmosphere that people on holiday demand. Your cousin Danny would ruin that."

"You're not kidding about the atmosphere. I've seen some lulus around that spring."

"I know."

"But I also noticed a lot of the old local yokels."

"They get to have it both ways. Their thing is to come just out of curiosity, night after night. I humor them. We elbow each other in the ribs. We point. They keep coming back. I specialize in catering to the big-spending local dipso. If I didn't have the out-of-towners, I'd have to hire topless dancers."

A long and awkward silence followed, maybe not awkward but full of something that brought pain without impatience. So it was a question of where it would end. Finally Lucien broke the quiet. "Why can't we just see each other in a normal kind of way?"

"Because we had that. And you left it. It has not returned just because we occupy the same real estate at the moment. I'm surprised you asked that question."

"You're surprised that I asked that question?"

"Yes, because it implies that I am either stupid or have no memory."

"I'm very much alone, Suzanne," Lucien said and was immediately sorry for even having tested this lame idea out loud. He received an actual Bronx cheer. "I'm coming over," he said and hung up.

When he got to the White Cottage, Suzanne let him in and said, "Will someone tell me why I'm even opening this door?" Lucien swept her into his arms and held her tight. His hands slid down over the roundness of her buttocks and felt them grow solid. He sensed himself getting suddenly hard. At least it will have something other to do than soak my foot through the top of my shoe, he thought confidently.

"I'm not going to fuck you," she said.

"Oh, yes you are."

"Oh, no I'm not." Her pelvis was firm and unmoving against him. He had never wanted to make love with anybody so much in his life. He couldn't remember how it had been with her because he had never really cared.

She planted the tips of her ten fingernails against his chest lightly and pushed him away. He glanced down. His nicely fitted slacks had a grim off-center bulge in them, and there was a spot too. Love.

Suzanne's eyes flickered away. Lucien remembered when she was a virgin. Virgins are bores, he thought, like people with overpriced houses. I suppose we could show you the living room; but we're not even sure we want to sell and we're very particular about the buyer. Lucien remembered Suzanne's virginity as something that one approached like a root canal. Against the precociously carnal Emily it seemed a little sappy.

So instead they had tea. Suzanne seemed so beautiful that Lucien stared too much and made gestures that were either not appropriate or off in their timing. The wind blew the door open and a strange dog came in while they watched. He drank from the spring and turned a gaunt brindle muzzle toward them coolly. When Lucien tried to shoo him, he merely watched, then left at his own speed, jogging angularly out through the door again.

⁘⁘⁘⁘⁘⁘⁘⁘⁘⁘⁘⁘⁘⁘⁘⁘⁘⁘⁘⁘⁘⁘⁘⁘⁘⁘⁘⁘⁘⁘⁘⁘⁘⁘⁘⁘⁘⁘⁘⁘⁘⁘⁘

The four nannies came up from Aspen in a chartered plane. Lucien met them and helped throw their numerous pieces of luggage into the carryall. The pilot barely emerged

# 15

from the cockpit to open the wing compartments. He looked like he had been through hell and seen all its famous inconveniences. He got back into the plane and stared saucer-eyed at the four ladies. The oldest of them, a girl of nearly thirty, wore an old prairie skirt and a T-shirt that said

ASPEN, COLORADO.
JEWS IN FOUR-WHEEL DRIVE.

The shirt made Lucien nervous. She took the lead conversationally and told Lucien that Montana was great, really great, she couldn't tell him how great. Two of the others looked to be sisters, early twenties, Eastern Mediterranean–looking. The last was almost silent, and when she remarked on what a nice day it was, she did so in an Australian accent. She wore Zuni jewelry and loud lipstick, hot pink. All bore the same high-strung, peaked quality that Lucien associated with the end of civilization as we know it.

He took them to the spring, checked them in and followed from a discreet distance as McCourtney showed them their rooms. Each tore into the contents of her luggage, then closed the door. It must have been very exciting luggage. The eldest nanny leaned out past McCourtney and called down the corridor to Lucien, "I'm Freddy. Ring me up when nothing's happening. I'm a light sleeper. And, you know, whatever."

Late that night Wick Tompkins came out and asked Lucien to have a drink with him. They sat off at one of the glass tables where you could hear the voices from the

133

spring and where you could imagine anything from being at sea to being at an old sanitarium in the Alps. Wick took out a cigarette and tapped it tight against the table, reversed it, tapped the other end and then set it between the edges of his teeth. He struck a match and gazed at Lucien.

"Remember that guy Emily ran off with?"

"W. T. Austinberry," said Lucien. "I do indeed."

Wick lit his cigarette. "Pretty-boy type."

"Only compared to us."

"What was your impression of him?"

"My impression? I don't know. Kind of a harmless cat, y'know. But not so bad. Why?"

"Smart?"

"Uh, not too smart."

"That's right," said Wick. "Not too smart."

"What are we driving at, Wick?"

"Emily shot him."

"Dead?"

"M-hm."

Lucien got the old sick heart back. He just wouldn't believe it. "Where is she?"

"Turks and Caicos."

"What's that?"

"A little island country."

"What's she doing there?"

"What else? Avoiding extradition."

"How do you know this, Wick?"

"Why, she called. She needs five thousand dollars. I gather that she has plenty of money but is embarrassed temporarily because of sudden moving."

Lucien wiggled his hand in the air for another round.

"Send it," he said. Then he gave his small smile that

meant the discussion was closed. Wick sighed in resignation and made himself a note.

"I love you, I hate you," said Wick. "But I can't save you from yourself."

It was quite late by the time Lucien walked Wick to his car. Wick looked back through the side window with a sad, uncomprehending smile and drove away, red taillights flicking on and off tentatively as Wick tried to make out the exit. Lucien went inside, wondering what terrible thing Austinberry must have done to make Emily take his life; absolutely no one was giving her a chance. She was like a deer being run by a pack of wild dogs.

He picked up the in-house phone and rang Freddy. He had feared waking her, but she was unbelievably wide awake. "Give me five minutes," she said. "Walk in and, whatever."

Lucien went behind the bar first and made himself a Stolie and tonic. He walked out to the edge of the spring. An elderly couple circled in each other's arms, dancing a musicless waltz in the night-blue depths like old and beautiful love on the rim of eternity. This is where we first made love, thought Lucien, my fugitive and I.

He sipped his way down the long corridor, carpeted for the comfort of wet bathers' feet, to Freddy's door. He finished his drink and leaned to set it next to the door. Inside he heard a vague hum like the sound of a transformer on a public building which has been shut up for the night. He went inside and there was Freddy, by God.

She was stretched out sideways on the bed, naked. The humming came from a gadget she had clutched to her genitals; her head hung upside down from the edge of

135

the bed. She opened her mouth wide and indicated its dark center with the long fingernail of her one free hand. You won't have to ask twice, thought Lucien, quickly undressing. He stepped over to Freddy and she manipulated him rigid without turning over. Lucien braced his knees on the mattress edge either side of her upside-down head. She stretched her tongue out far and wide. Whatever, thought Lucien mirthlessly, and slid himself all the way down her throat. He was able to glide freely in and out before her thrilling epiglottal clench drove an orgasm up through him. He fell forward on his hands to steady himself through the spasms; and heard the heated giggling from underneath. In a moment he dragged himself from Freddy as her glistening mouth closed in a kind of backward kiss. He went down on his knees and peered under the bed. There were the three little faces of the Aspen nannies.

"Just what sort of people are you?" he asked.

He woke up the next morning, made breakfast and brought it back to bed with him. This morning he let Sadie get in bed with him. That was a Sunday morning privilege and ceremony, when he would read the previous Sunday's New York *Times*. Sadie always spotted the plastic mail wrapping and knew it was her day. Today was Thursday and Lucien had gotten four days behind; but Sadie didn't know that, so today she got bed privileges and finger-held fragments of bacon and egg whites. People wondered why he didn't build a better home to go with his new prosperity; but this old house suited Lucien fine. It was two ranges of hills from the hot spring, an increasingly important factor of insulation.

He cradled the phone against his shoulder, scanned

"The Week in Review," and dialed Antoinette. "Anybody looking for me?"

"The coroner's office."

"The coroner's office . . ."

"They want to know what to do with Kelsey."

"I don't know and I don't care," said Lucien, grabbing the phone in his hand. "*Wait a minute*," he shouted. Sadie jumped off the bed. "Call the coroner back and tell him you talked to me. Tell him I said there was no such fucking thing as Kelsey. You got that? Just tell him so he knows: *There's no Kelsey*." He hung up and waited until his breathing was normal before he went back to his paper.

As luck would have it, Turks and Caicos was in the paper. Apparently it was a cluster of islands in the eastern Bahamas. Apparently it was all beaches and banks where dope dealers and Vesco types stored their money. There was a picture of a palm-shaded beach with a lethal-looking cigarette boat in the foreground and a modern slab of a bank in the background. Lucien knew Emily's taste, he thought, enough to think she'd find this beach scene tacky and shallow. It saddened him to imagine her hurrying up the crushed coral walk and pushing through the plate-glass door to the air-conditioned room that held the five thousand he'd sent.

He got up to dress. Sadie jumped on and off the bed till he looked over at her and she stopped. He really didn't know how to dress; whether to dress for his guests or to dress for the plumbing repairs he had to make on the mixing valves beneath the spring. Maybe a flight suit to symbolize either getting out of town or aiding Emily in her banking would have been on the nose. Maybe a diaper.

The mail contained an eight-by-ten envelope from Wick Tompkins. Now, this was suspicious. Lucien hardly ever knew Wick to use the mail to him. Wick's hand deliveries of trifling papers were part of their life together. The contents of the envelope were simple and eloquent: a Uruguayan police photograph of W. T. Austinberry with a bullet hole in his left eye socket. The face had been scrubbed free of blood, the right lid tucked in place. The horrid gap nearly obscured the identity of Austinberry, but somehow the vaguely cowboy Scots-Irish face remained his.

Lucien went to the phone.

"Where did you get the picture?"

"The police here in town."

"What were they doing with it?"

"Helping verify who it was."

"Well, it's him."

"It sure is. Wouldn't you venture he'd kind of lost his looks?"

"I'd like to know what he did to deserve it, Wick. That's what I'd like to know."

There was a long pause.

"Lucien," said Wick. "Don't do this to me."


Lucien stopped down at Dominic Armada's room. By keeping the room year-round—and he never asked for a rate—Dominic had transformed it into his own single flat, with

# 16

none of the atmosphere of a hotel or spa. The room smelled of Ben-Gay and garlic; the beady-eyed Madonnas stood along the wall like duck decoys. There was a photograph of the bay of Naples that made Lucien long suddenly and irrationally for the sea, a longing that ended abruptly with a memory of the island church where Lord Nelson was married and where Lucien raised questions about his life that he still had not answered.

"Siddown, siddown, siddown, Lucien," said the old penitent. Lucien sat on one of the Miami lawn chairs Dominic had brought for its associations and drank wine from a highball glass. Lucien immediately entered into the sort of urbanized character he became around Dominic; it was a relief to be that person for a moment.

"Lucien, sell me this hot spring, please."

"You've got a nice room, Dom. That's enough. This place is my pride and joy."

Lucien realized that Dominic wished to pass his declining days among vaguely genteel people, defending his Madonnas against the occasional drunk who got the wrong door. Dominic's laughter displayed his long teeth, and on Saturday night he always sent down a hundred dollars to buy a round of drinks for "the nice cowboys in the bar. And their gals." Dominic had first drawn Lucien into conversation by explaining to him that he had spent many years in the horse business. When Lucien asked him where, he said, "The fifty-dollar window."

Dominic's phone rang. "Yeah, he's here." He reached it to Lucien.

"I'll take it in my office," Lucien said to Antoinette. "Gotta go, Dom." He chugged the red wine.

"I could help you." Dominic smiled. "Keep the headache."

Lucien walked toward his office, imagining the solid squeeze the pale hold button had on the caller. He was not in a hurry. It seemed he alternated regularly between a placid acceptance of the need to be normal, to get, spend and lay waste; and the sense that his time was the only true coinage and he was misspending it and death was creeping at him on little cat feet.

"Darling?"

"Yes?"

"It's Emily."

"Emily!"

His nerve net became a skein of heated platinum wire. How different this terror and desire seemed in the face of a platitudinous day barely saved by the epiglottal clamp of Freddy. Lucien stretched the coiled telephone cord to get the door open and admit Sadie, a fine bird dog who had become a poolside whore in Lucien's newest life. Sadie jumped repeatedly over Lucien's desk while he talked.

"Are you doing all right?" Emily asked through clouds of Caribbean static.

"Maybe too well," Lucien shouted nervously. "I've overstabilized the risk factor." Suddenly he was uneasy for having said that. What did she want? What did she want of him?

"Well, I'm only calling to say thanks. You've been terribly generous. And I'm fine, I'm going to be okay. Don't worry about me, Lucien, okay?" The static arose, making palpable all that distance, all that southerliness and ocean distance. And finally it swallowed Emily.

"Where are you?" Lucien asked in an excited voice as Sadie sized up the filing cabinet. "Emily, where *are* you?"

Lucien buzzed Antoinette.

"Antoinette, did you get a call-back number on that last one?"

"No, I didn't."

"Why not?"

"Why not? Because you came to the phone, Mr. Taylor."

"Ah, so I did."

"Are you all right?"

"That's what the lady who called just asked. Is there something wrong with my voice?"

"No, I—"

"Would you like me to intone something in a lower register in order to prevent these inquiries as to my well-being?"

Monday and Tuesday were spent with the accountant. The spring was at a kind of financial income limit. The question was toward the write-offs now, or an outright sale. All the little things, raising the rates, improving the dining room and its revenues, adding services, were fairly well used up. And besides that, the concessionaires, if you could call them that, noting the stability of the business through advance bookings and other sensors, wanted raises. Mary Celeste was particularly bad about that: she viewed Workmen's Compensation as a neglected gold mine. Lucien was afraid to tell her that for every person who was drawn to her therapy there were two who were appalled at sending feces across the wall in glass tubes; so he gave her a raise and she sulked off in her caftan. The accountant, Dan Janoff, stared at his sheets and made itchy traceries on his bald spot with the point of his pencil.

"I'd say—let me look at this now—I'd say you're either going to have to sell it or just view it as an ongoing money machine, which won't change and which—I know you—won't be *that* exciting as a business *qua* life passion."

"You're wrong about that. It's very exciting. I'm happier than you think."

"So long as you emphasize your losses, losses are valuable things. Sell them to yourself before they are captured by someone less worthy. Everyone is trying to buy losses. These days it's the sizzle, not the steak."

A short time later Janoff gathered his paperwork to his chest and went out. When Lucien heard his BMW grind off through the deep gravel, he got up, thinking what a nice place he had created for himself and for others. It *would* be hard to give up. He got to his feet and walked out into the evening air, feeling a warm inversion come down the mountain and across his face.

But then, by force of will, Lucien behaved as usual for his dinner guests. Scrubbed and cologned, he made his way through the dining room, circled the old spring twice, made thoughtful moues to his concessionaires and returned to his office with its pictures of his parents and his child. He worked there and fell asleep at the desk on purpose. Some hours later, awakened by his alarm watch, Lucien rose and made his rounds of the spring. He went over the books in front and the bar receipts when the last celebrant had gone to his room. He'd usually exchange a few convivial words with the night watchman, light a cigar and stroll the flagstone shore of the spring. But tonight, late tonight, with the prospect of Kelsey emerging again and again, he sat down beside the empty spring and watched the phantoms drift toward the skylights and walls. He remembered when he and his father had first seen the spring under a mantle of circling crows. But he remembered too being there with Emily. And he felt his throat ache. He didn't know if it was from remembering his father, from remembering Emily, or because the spring had become a bit of a madhouse. If it was the latter, he'd get over it; for, despite his adoration of the natural world, he despised the quiet life. It was better for the spring to draw the successful, those in need, the hungry, the full, the kings and queens of boogie, the mindless and desperate, than just lie there. Lucien was not ashamed; he just wasn't sure why he was so blue.

Wick called Lucien at the spring. Lucien was out at poolside fielding complaints. One man demanded to go "downstairs" and adjust the mixing valve, as it was too hot in the pool. Lucien explained that it came straight out of the ground at one hundred fifteen degrees. "And after you adjust the mixing valve," the man replied, "add chlorine." Lucien advised him that it was considered a marvel that the state found the water so clean that additives were not required. "The chlorine'll get after those bugs," the man said conclusively and left.

"Saw Suzanne," said Wick.

"And?"

"I strongly advise you to throw yourself at her feet and beg for another chance."

"She's something, isn't she."

"Why don't you stop by my Chinese restaurant and share a quiet litchi. I can go over the QED on that topic and spare you from endlessly shooting yourself in the foot."

"Fuck you, I'm a millionaire."

"Today I'm having tea-smoked duck and some nice Mexican welterweights via the satellite dish to help pass the time. Too, there is a pleasant view of the Deadrock skyline and the music of our nearby switching yard."

"I can't make it. I'm going to try to pick up on stuff here."

"Incidentally, by way of deepening your debt to me, I handled your Kelsey problem. I donated him to a college in North Dakota. I had him tagged and shipped. I'm going to let the college deal directly with the family on any complications there might be involved, and I billed them for the freight, the embalming and that snazzy container. The wife called and got snarky with me. So if there's any problem on collecting, I'll garnishee their damn television set. I know how to hate too."

"I can't thank you enough for handling that. I never thought I'd see the last of him. Not that he wasn't a nice guy. However, this thing went on and on."

"But remember, if you ever need a liver transplant or anything, we've got an inside line at the college."

"Goodbye, Wick."


Life and death, thought Lucien. That's all I have to say. One minute you're shipping a body, the next you're beating your brains out trying to get into some housewife's shorts. During Lucien's bad winter he had pulled his friend Dee into the unlocked foyer, a kind of anteroom in front of the locked plate-glass doors, of the Deadrock First Security Bank; whereupon like two rumpled suits they made long and boisterous love. The next day the large staff of the bank reviewed the activity on their video surveillance system. The time ran on the right-hand side of the screen, grimly factoring Lucien's performance.

144

Once again, Lucien's dick had dragged him someplace the rest of him would never have gone alone, and caused him shame.

At two the mayor, Donald Deems, came in with his secretary and tossed down a hollow-sounding briefcase. His secretary was lean and large-boned as Don Quixote, and she worked hyperkinetically in her steno book and stared out of the window to the hot spring. There were three or four local schoolteachers in the pool, bobbing and chatting amiably. Sometimes Lucien's former math teacher, Mrs. Hunt, came and glowered in the shallow end, looking for her old victims. I ought to pound that geek, thought Lucien.

"What've you got going today, Donald?"

"We've got the sister-city deal, Lucien. You remember."

"I do remember but I don't know what to do different. We're ready for them. It's what, half a dozen people?"

"No, more than that. I don't even know what country they're from, but it's Deadrock's sister city. Someplace out in the Pacific with one syllable. Zook, Plock, something, I don't know. Don't write that down, for Christ's sakes!" he said to the scribbling secretary. He fingered the skip-stitching in his lapel.

"Do they speak any English?"

"I don't know, Lucien. Foreign aid and papaya is their main deal, I guess."

"Well, we'll sure try to make them feel at home. If we only knew what home was—"

"I just thought, you being in the State Department . . ."

"Do you know what letter it starts with?"

"I'll find out, I'll find out."

"Maybe you could go through some back issues of the *National Geographic*."

The mayor bobbed his chin and looked off pensively. "I know it's somewheres out there in the Pacific somewheres."

Suzanne appeared briefly in the window, her brown eyes bright against a new tan. She gave Lucien a small wave in which he was more than a little suspicious there was flirting. He raised his arm toward the mayor in a kind of stiff-arm gesture and darted for the door. By the time he got out to the pool, Suzanne had gone past the far end, wearing a cotton wrap over her bathing suit. By now she was strolling with a tall young man, a college student possibly; and the two of them turned into the open bar. Lucien would have raced after them and spoken to her, but he knew he had almost no chance of appearing self-possessed; and he had perfect capability for imagining himself looking very awkward indeed in front of . . . the two of them. He went back into the office.

"Is something the matter?" the mayor asked, his secretary standing by to write down the answer.

"No, someone I know."

"You look sick."

Lucien cut through this. "Where were we?" he asked.

"We were through. Don't let us hold you."

"I've got it all down," said the secretary. The two of them were ready to go now, but they still seemed to want to watch Lucien. There was something about Lucien they couldn't keep their eyes off.

When the mayor had gone, Lucien stretched out on the couch. He thought back upon happy times with Suzanne. There had been the fall before James was born when they had the cruising sloop. Lucien worked then in the Dominican Republic, distributing leaflets to

Latinos. They spent all their free time sailing, and Lucien took a mail-order course in celestial navigation. He remembered a successful night landing with pride to this day. There was enough moon when they reached St. Barthélemy that they could make Baie de St. Jean by putting the stern on Isle Bonhomme and running for the grove of palms, one of which had been striped white as a monument. Soon they heard the reef pass behind the white of the mainsail. Lucien rounded up and they anchored. Suddenly it was still. The lights from shore caught the curl going down the reef, but the surf could no longer be heard. Suzanne furled the sails carefully and Lucien secured the wheel so the rudder wouldn't knock in the night. They went below and made love while the VHF radio crackled with island conversations. The riding light appeared and disappeared over one port-hole with the slight running swell. Lucien awoke in the morning to see Suzanne making coffee in the small galley wearing only the bottom of her bathing suit. A warm, fragrant breath of the island came down the companionway; from a distance he could hear the small French motorcars. That night they stayed up late in one of the local bars and ended by renting a room in a cottage that faced an old compound of houses. There was a wooden water tower surmounted by a salvaged ship's water tank, strangely shaped on this support, as it had been made to fit in the bow of a vessel. Water was pumped up to it from a cistern and allowed to fall by gravity into the cottage's water system. Lucien propped the door shut with a chunk of porous local rock. Trumpet vines lay up against the panes of blueing window glass, and the palm trees moved slowly in the oceanic wind. Suzanne and Lucien lay in each other's arms.

Lucien was asleep on the couch.

Suzanne sent James over to have break- **17** fast with his father. There was an alcove next to the spring, where they sat to- gether and listened in on conversations at the nearby tables. An older lady talked in a high voice. "It was either this place or the *QE II*. But there had been talk in the press about the stabilizers failing and tummy upset at the captain's table. So we came here. I like it. I think I like it. Do you like it?" Her companion, another woman her own age, flicked her eyes in Lucien's direction to signal that he was listening, and things murmured to a stop.

Little James had his head tilted back as though he needed bifocals; he was holding a piece of toast that looked half the size of his head, and he was just smiling at his father without fear for the first time since his arrival. His shirt was one button out of line and Lucien leaned across and made it right. Lucien wondered how in God's name he could ever leave the boy unguarded even for a moment, much less for the duration of his recent hegira. "Self-discovery," he thought with loathing, for he was losing interest in himself. He wished now he could install his wasted years as unused time in his little boy's life. It was a kind of regret.

"I hope we'll fish a little."

"That'd be great," said James anxiously.

"You like sport, though . . . ?"

"Not athletics!"

"This is different. You can go off and be to yourself.

148

When I was your age, people used to hang out gone-fishing signs and they never had to explain anything. Just go look at the air or find out what's out past the trees. You can still do that."

"I can?"

"Sure you can."

From another table came an implacable voice: "When that Ford tipped over, it took a Jaws of Life to set me free. I'm a lucky man to be here to tell about it."

"If we fish," said James, knitting his fingers in his lap, "I don't care if we get one."

"I don't either."

"But I hope we get one."

"Me too."

Lucien ate the same thing he'd eaten for thousands of mornings: bacon and eggs and hash browns, with hot sauce on the eggs. He looked at them and wondered if they were the only continuity he had. As he stared down, there was a moment of complete suspension in which the sound of silverware and morning voices poured through eternity like a river. I want an island, he thought; I want an island.

The year Lucien and Suzanne parted, they had gone up to the States for the usual minor supplies: paperbacks, a cordless electric razor, Suzanne's contacts, ten or twenty movies, a pump for the saltwater aquarium. It was the year they had both come out of the mall with things that seemed to bode ill for the future: Suzanne with a pair of crotchless panties, Lucien with his first corncob pipe. It proved to be a very bad sign indeed, especially since Lucien was in an epoch when it seemed to him there actually were *signs*, an era in which he could join the

149

rest of the populace in the wonderful ongoing melodrama of inanimate objects. He thrilled to clothes and cars; he sat at an old tropical wicker desk which seemed to guarantee character in his work. It was also the time he began to feel that his dick had rights of its own. He viewed it the way Vasco da Gama viewed the needle of his compass. Wherever he went, he believed it to be one of the leading dicks in the area. He never wanted to be accused of standing in its way. It was an up-market dick even when it spotted his clothes, made a crude lump or pissed through the top of his shoes. Still, the real story lay in his sense of getting nowhere, the functionary blues.

The voice at the other end said, "I'm told you can put me in touch with Suzanne Taylor." It was a man.

"I think I can. What's it about?"

"It's about when she's coming back to work."

"Isn't this kind of a vacation for her?" Lucien asked. He was racking his brain to recall what the job was: something about life-insurance money and land investment in the Sunbelt. His part of the office did Houston to Memphis, and she worked in his division.

"It'd just be real nice to hear when she is planning to pop up."

"I think she's trying for a couple of weeks holiday with her little boy."

"It won't do. You tell her to get hold of Lawton Hudson. That's me. Tell her I said now is the hour."

Lawton Hudson clicked off. Lucien had felt unable to put in his two cents' worth fearing he'd jeopardize something he knew nothing about. But he was furious.

He spoke to no one as he made his rounds. In the kitchen, they looked at him from the steam of breakfast dishes. Henchcliff was receiving meats, checking them off as they were transferred to the trolley in cold storage. There were the usual newspaper readers at the pastry table who jumped up when Lucien came in. Along the poolside, three or four men made notes in their half-glasses, looking up with that peculiar air of dubiety which those glasses produce. One of the nannies was backed up tight to the water intake, absolutely oblivious to Lucien or anything else. The bar was still locked, and the morning light was just making it to the high windows and beaming down on the continually changing pool of thermal water. Once when they were first open, a local rancher had galloped his horse into the pool and gone to the bar for a drink. There had been something of a struggle to prevent the horse from drowning. Afterward Lucien took a chair to the rancher. The rancher had not come back since, though his lawyer made two or three sheepish calls.

Antoinette was taking reservations at a good clip, and the front office was filled with the wonderful smell of hot asphalt from the pavers outside. There was a warm breeze coming through the open windows, and Lucien could hear the American flag pop over the parking lot. Antoinette touched her forefinger to the dimple in her right cheek and bethought herself while the phone flashed. In the lobby a local decorator hung pictures of windmills, buckaroos, roundups and amazingly smoky trains. A smooth operation, Lucien thought.

"Antoinette, has Miss Taylor arranged for any activities for my son today?"

"I believe he has a riding lesson in half an hour. At ten."

"I see. I didn't know that. Who's giving the lesson?"

"I believe it's Sheila."

"Antoinette, get Sheila and make sure the lesson lasts a couple of hours. Sheila is to teach James riding for two hours."

Now Lucien began to move rapidly. From the tennis courts, he could see down to the stables. Sheila was lecturing James about the parts of a saddle while James sat up on a tall bay horse that seemed to be sleeping through the lecture.

Then he walked through the grove of flowering crab apples to the White Cottage. When he got to the wall, he walked around to the side that faced open country and stopped to level his breathing. Then he climbed the timber crossbrace of the wall and looked inside the court. As he expected, Suzanne was sunbathing beside the pool. For some reason he was startled by the lankiness of her naked body. She had one arm crooked over her face, and her breathing was slow and rhythmic. Once the arm swung out suddenly as though at a fly, and the effect of that on Lucien was a kind of fright. One knee was angled slightly against the other, drawing up one long curve of thigh. Lucien couldn't help studying to see if her breasts had fallen; they hadn't. Then she sat up and thought for a moment; he was afraid to move. She walked to the table and made a long-distance phone call; he knew this because he counted the digits and there were eleven altogether. Long-distance. She leaned onto her elbows with her fingers run into her auburn hair and talked and laughed for a few minutes. Then she hung up. As she walked back to the pool she kept smiling from the phone conversation and lay down again.

When he climbed back down he felt tremulous. He had the key to the gate and he walked around to the door.

152

He touched the end of the key to the opening in the lock, waited a moment, then pushed very slowly, feeling each notch fall softly along the shaft of the key. He turned it and the door went loose. He stepped in. Now he was looking straight at Suzanne from a very short distance, unnoticed.

When he held her wrists and kissed her, her scream went all the way down his throat. Then she knew it was him and stopped. She just looked at him, resting on her elbows, with not the beginning of an expression. Lucien undressed and moved her knees apart with his own. He stopped then and waited. A second later, she crammed him inside her and he felt tears on her cheeks. It should have ruined things, but Suzanne's healthy animalism was something she could never entirely eliminate, and they made love for a long time.

"Why have you done this?"

"I couldn't help it."

"Right."

"I was sort of crazy. I'm not kidding, darling. I was controlled by something else—" He was telling the truth.

"A sort of lever."

"Please."

"*Please.* I can't believe you'd say that to me. What could be more adorable, Lucien, than your put-upon air?"

"You lubricated."

"I ask you, please stop. That's how they defend rapists."

"And your boss called, wants you back at work yesterday."

"There's another thing we haven't touched on. My work. Anyway, let's not quarrel. James'll be here in a minute."

"Not to worry. He's having a two-hour lesson."

153

"Isn't that thoughtful. You moved him into a larger time slot." She was getting angry.

"You didn't have to make love with me," Lucien said petulantly.

"That's right, I didn't. But I hadn't fucked anybody in about a week. I must've needed it."

"Please don't talk that way."

"I'll talk any way I please. I'm just a working mother and I've got my shoulder to the wheel, you sonofabitch."

"Whooo."

"You know what," she said with blazing eyes, "I think I hate you. Why don't you go fuck something else. I don't think I want to fuck you anymore. Yeah, that's it. No more fucking you, and here's why: it encourages all your sloppy sentimentality and your no-shows and your desertions and your treatment of people who love you as if they were so many pocket mirrors for you to see if you're aging or what kind of day you're having or how deep and creative you are or how effective and memorable your personal philosophy is or whether you might not start going back to church or how many months it was since your last complete physical or whether you ought to give up after-dinner drinks. No, you sonofabitch, I don't think I'll fuck you anymore. I think I'll just get the hell out of here and fuck someone else. You know how it goes."

Lucien left. He was astounded at Suzanne's description and the depth of her feeling. He had a drink at the bar, drove two buckets of balls at the driving range, shucked half a dozen air-fresh Chesapeake oysters with his personal prying iron, ate them, made ten or twenty effective business calls and bought James a fishing rod. He just wished he had Suzanne and that they were back on the Gulf Stream in a light norther in their old sloop bound for glory. He wished he were still playing third base, guarding the hot corner all those summers ago. Principally, he was exhilarated by her rage.

But it seemed to be true: she hated him.

"Antoinette," he said a while later, "get the number, the long-distance call, Suzanne made from the White Cottage around half past ten. Then put a call through for me to that number."

He waited as it rang and then was answered. It was the man who had called. "Yeah," said Lucien. "I got you an answer on Suzanne Taylor's return to work. She'll get there when she gets there. Okay? She'll get there when she gets there."

"I think this is very sad for you," the man said. "I'd hate to be in your position."

•-•-•-•-•-•-•-•-•-•-•-•-•-•-•-•-•-•-•-•-•-•-•-•-•-•-•-•-•-•-•-•-•-•-•-•-•-•-•-•-•-•-•-•

Things at the spring grew very busy without warning. The Elks booked two luncheons, which on top of the built-in traffic made things burdensome. Nor was Henchcliff taking it as well as he might have. "Lucien," he said after the second day of this, "we had a very specific conversation about what was expected of me and what was expected of me the way I saw it was high-grade, high-priced cooking, which cannot be done at the same rate as franks and beans. I don't see this as an eatery."

"I know that. But bear with us, we're in business here. We've got to take it as it comes."

"*You* have to take it as it comes. I'm a cook, I'm an artist."

"No," said Lucien. "Cooks are not artists. Somebody should have explained that to you."

Henchcliff pushed his hands deep into his pockets and bucked his elbows in close to his ribs: heavy weather ahead. "You want to spend a couple days with me in front of that oven?"

"I pay you to do that. Plus I'm the wrong guy to be having this conversation. I don't give a shit what people put in their goddamn mouths. In fact, long conversations about what people put in their mouths bore the hell out of me. I've got plenty of problems of my own right now, Hench. It's not like I'm interested in trying yours on for size. Why don't you quit crying and go to work?"

Antoinette, on the other hand, was booking them hand over fist. She really thrived on pressure. If it slacked off, she went creative, and that's where trouble began. Now, seeing her bent grimly at her ledger, Lucien felt a flood of warmth that watching loyalty produces. He of course knew it was illusory, but what wasn't. He leaned over and gave her a serious hug.

He checked the linen carts and occupancy list; there was a Billings car in staff parking and he had it towed. He had Shane paint out the graffiti in the bar men's room and he checked the liquor inventory against the bartender's sheet. The olives were down. The tar had firmed up in the parking lot, so he took down the rope and flags that cordoned it off. There were three trucks with white-water rafts slung up in their beds waiting to park, and he waved to the drivers as they moved onto the new tar with an adhesive sound. He filled the bird-feeders and did up the wire ties on the garbage bags behind the kitchen. He ran a stick up into the mouths of the six drainspouts and dislodged leaves and sculch. Four of the six ran copious water though it was a sunny day. Seamless gutters. He threw a tarp over the log-splitter and pulled the rolling doors shut in the front of the tractor shed. He had all the fiery cheer of a man with a family business.

He skipped his dinner and worked until dark. His muscles ached and he took a long shower to feel better. That night Suzanne let him stay. The clean, painted white walls of the room made their shadows vivid; and beyond the door he could see James sound asleep on the daybed with true stories of the American West piled by his side.

"James, what are you interested in?" Lucien had the willows bent down and he was trying to dislodge James's trout fly. James put his fly in the brush more than he put it in the water.

"A lot of things."

"What are you best at?"

"What?"

"What do you do the best?"

"Aren't I going to find out from you?" asked James.

The stream wound through brush in open country. There were antelope off near the limits of visibility, and rising and settling clouds of blackbirds. The pools were sandy and the trout hovered in small schools like fish in the ocean.

The next day a small thing happened which Lucien took to be a sign, a good sign. He went to town ostensibly to do some banking but really because the luncheon special at the Part Time Bar was split-pea soup, Lucien's favorite. All municipal matters were being settled in the booths and along the counter. The poker machines had until Friday to get out of town, and most people seemed glad to see them go. Two cowboys were disputing whether or not Tom Horn really shot the kid, and withal, there was an atmosphere of time arrested for an appropriate review period or just a decorous tableau. But the sign actually was Dee, Lucien's old squeeze, with a booth of her own. Lucien sat down. She was wearing her jeans and a pink sleeveless sweater. She was attractive. No wonder I was always sticking my dick in her, thought Lucien.

"Guess what?"

"I can't," said Lucien.

"I'm leaving Shit-for-Brains."

"Hasn't he been a good husband to you?" Lucien asked, knowing right away that it would have been darned hard to say anything sillier. He ordered the soup.

"You'll also be delighted to hear I'm leaving town."

"I'm not delighted to hear that."

"We found ways of passing the time," she said. "Me and you."

"We certainly did."

"My sister's a florist in Salt Lake," she said. "They've got a video dish. I can stay with them until I learn the ropes. I don't know squat about flowers. But then, what did you know about hot springs?"

"Nothing," agreed Lucien quickly.

"You just fucked the right murderer."

"Ha ha ha."

"What's funny? With me it was a gutter salesman. But I can't take it anymore. Wednesday he got one of these electric garage doors, and we haven't been able to get the car out for three days. I walked downtown. So that's it for me. I don't care how many Mormons Salt Lake's got. I've had a picture of that seagull since sixth grade and I knew someday I'd go. Also, Shit-for-Brains is about to receive news of foreclosure and I don't want to be standing there when that one hits. It's real simple around our place: I want to be somebody and he wants to be nobody. It's just exactly that black and white. I'm gonna go down to Salt Lake with all those Mormons and sleep my way to the top."

"It's hard to think of the right thing to say, Dee."

"Why say anything? You've got it made. But remember this, old Dee was there when you were walking the hoot-owl trail."

That night Lucien played checkers with James and lost. The little boy sat in a plaid bathrobe and carpet slippers —where did children get carpet slippers these days?— and played to win; Lucien couldn't stop him. Lucien helped Suzanne put him to bed; she'd bought him a globe during the day and he twirled it slowly as he drifted off murmuring the names of the countries. They made love and Lucien fell asleep thinking about Dee out on that highway; she probably took a few pills to get the trip behind her.

Sometime late, in the middle of the night, Suzanne got up and said she could hear the brindle dog drinking out of the pool. Lucien asked what difference it made. "I guess none," said Suzanne. "Doesn't anyone own him?" Lucien threw his head back on the pillow because somehow Suzanne had made it seem such a despairing question. "I thought if I chased him away from our pool he'd go home. But that doesn't necessarily follow if he has no home."

"Suzanne, please stop this."

"I will. I'm going on and on, aren't I?"

"A little."

"Am I okay to make love with?" Suzanne asked.

"What do you think?"

"Well, you were never like this with me before. I think you want me."

"I do," said Lucien.

"I mean, more than before."

"Something was the matter with me before," said Lucien.

"That's not the matter with you now?"

"Here's hoping," said Lucien.

"*Here's hoping!*"

"I didn't mean that. I just didn't want to jinx myself. I know we're happy, a bit at least. I'm thinking, little steps for little feet. All I'd need is some jinx now and that would about do it."

Lucien wondered about her work. He knew that there would be a certain lingering foulness about his enquiring as to her relationship with her employer. And besides, he was briefly bored by matters of sexual envy. It was like talking endlessly about the toothed holes in people's faces through which they passed pieces of food. Finally, enough was enough, though the variegated impulses continued to leave a ranker scent trail than the most ancient jackal. In the end, one was put off by the body itself, a virtual Kelsey, suitable for donation to some godforsaken college. One wanted the brain, a pure sensorium, flying around without weight. The poor old dick was continually fighting gravity: making trouble in resistance, falling down the wrong pant-leg in remission. Younger owners each considered his a lordly shlong; but finally it is seen for what it is, a little maniac.

There was a bedside lamp, and Lucien wrote their initials in the light covering of dust, thinking, I do in fact love this girl. When she fell asleep once more, he got up quietly and went in to look at James. It seemed to Lucien that children took up great space when they were awake and then became so small when they fell asleep. James looked completely different because he did not wear his thick glasses. The odd way in which he hovered within his own clothes was replaced by a carelessness that relieved Lucien as he looked at the boy. It was as though James could someday emerge from his frightened self and go on and be happy and maybe through some as yet undiscovered process lay claim to the years his father misused. Lucien knew perfectly well that this last thought was completely foolish; but it gave him peace and he was able to sleep immediately, as people with self-respect are said to do.

Sweet is fleet. They could pick up and go. They were their own society. They could go back to Green Turtle and take the place at Black Sound. Lucien could even paint a little. James could collect hermit crabs out of the mangrove roots for bonefish bait and they could run down to Manjack and fish the flats. Or back in the USIA! In many ways that was an interesting job, all right, and he could get back to it before he lost his Spanish for good. Anything was possible once the center had been restored. Not that Lucien was thinking there were anything less than countless scars from the past, near and far. He thought now he could get over Emily, as he had seen her for what she was and she was out of the question, and she was gone. Obviously that all made him sad, but her chain of bad luck seemed something he lacked the power to break. If that was fatalism, then it would have to be. Nor would he brood about Suzanne's interim love life. Certain things had become tedious, and watching himself start over again like a cat on perpetual linoleum was something he would do no more.

They had to get an ambulance for one of the nannies. She just wouldn't wake up. She had paid off housekeeping to stay out of her way, and there were all sorts of food scraps from the kitchen that had to be cleared out. She woke up at the hospital and was vacationing again in a few hours with the Australian nanny, who looked like she herself would conk out in a matter of a few more hours. All the nannies were on some kind of marathon; two of them could take it and keep on eating and, clearly, two couldn't.

Lucien drove his truck into Deadrock for a cortisone shot. During the long winter alone, he had actually gotten tennis elbow from self-abuse. Now it wouldn't go away and he was accepting treatment. His doctor, of course, tried to have a discussion about larger health issues. Lucien scotched that.

"I'd like you to pay a little closer attention to your health. This is the middle of your life," said the doctor.

"You got that right. And it runs about a hundred years in length with record-breaking happy stretches. . . . Pump that sonofabitch. I'm a working man with a family to support."

Then he took a walk through the streets of Deadrock, retracing a few childhood paths, remembering places where dogs got him on his paper route, and seeing the fine big houses, as well as the small homes in which there was owner pride; the different buildings where his father had had offices and the small pharmacies where his mother had secured wacky prescriptions and home-permanent kits. There were kids running along the side-walk, many of them the kind of reasonably comely youths in which an already typed and crude adult can be seen. He saw where he learned to play third base and where he lost a big fight with his best friend and where he made his first wages pumping gas and working for a roofer. He could still remember leaving an unfinished brake job, the sedan up on the hoist, to go off and try to be a cowboy in the hills around town. He stayed away from the house where he had lived with his mother. Was it like women and childbirth in that the pain was not remembered? He still loved the place and saw no reason that you could not live there and always be happy.

He drove back to the house. When he went inside, Emily was sitting at the table reading the local paper. "I brought you a coconut from where the trade winds blow," she said.

"You did?" he said vacantly.

"I put it on your side of the bed," said Emily. Her hair was bleached bone-white and only her eyes were made up. She had a thin, hell-bent air.

"So!" said Lucien in a tone of discovery. "You're back."

By five Lucien was at the airport with the mayor, the city officials of Deadrock, a handful of community leaders and **19** prominent ranchers, a Production Credit Association man, a trio from the Chamber of Commerce, one woman from the Better Business Bureau and the Deadrock High School band. Lucien still did not have the correct name of the sister city, but its delegation stuck out like a sore thumb climbing off the airplane. For one thing, they were tiny people and wore dresses or sarongs that swept the tarmac; you couldn't tell the men from the women, and until one of them stepped forward at the end, there seemed to be no order to their arrival. They merely swept off the plane and moved haphazardly around the runway. One of the baggage handlers shooed them along toward the terminal. Once they got inside, an old man not much more than four feet high made a speech in his native tongue, a coursing of percussive notes across an unfathomable scale. A couple of the ranchers took it upon themselves to herd these people into the waiting cars. Lucien was not much help. In fact, the mayor studied him for a moment and asked, "Cat got your tongue?" Lucien shook his head quickly, then listened as the leader of the delegation from wherever it was said in perfect English, "We got jet lag. Time to sack out." The line of cars strung along the interstate toward Deadrock and the hot spring.

Lucien watched the guests receive the delegation. Everyone was at poolside to observe the little people. Quite suddenly about half the delegation pulled off their sarongs; they were wearing cloths knotted about their loins, and they sprang into the pool, where they shot around like marine animals, hardly struggling but moving at what seemed an unnatural speed through the water. Some of them had larger breasts than the others and must have been women. Lucien used the house phone to call Suzanne.

"Hi, darling, I'm over at the spring. Look, I don't know how long this is going to be going on. I think I'll just kind of tough it out and stay at my house."

"Have you taken something?"

"Taken something?"

"You sound as though you had taken something."

"God no, I wish I had. I've just got my hands full here. Look, I'll spell this out later."

"I love you."

"You do?"

"I sure do," she said. "James is listening to me and pointing to himself and saying, 'Me too.' "

"Oh, my lord," said Lucien.

Emily turned off the television and looked at Lucien coming into the living room. "I just saw you with all those dwarfs on TV. What country is that, for crying out loud?"

"I wish I knew."

"You can tell they're foreign as hell," said Emily "But that's the first time I saw how you'd fixed up the spring. I mean, I expected a lot, but you've been a busy beaver, haven't you?" She smiled at him fixedly. The room was filled with her perfume, a smell Lucien remembered as a fragrance favored in the big cities of Central America. "Have you turned over a new leaf?"

"Why are you wearing so much eye makeup?"

"Answer mine first."

"Yeah," said Lucien. "I have."

"Well, it's sort of a new me too. The best of the old and the best of the new. If you're not crazy about it, you get a refund at the door."

"At the door?"

"At the door."

She went into the downstairs bedroom and began throwing things into piles on the floor. "I want to take a dip in my old swimming hole. *Es posible?*"

"Of course."

"Well, that's fine, because I do want to do that. Maybe later, after the dwarfs are sleeping."

"They're just small. They're not dwarfs."

"Shall we measure them? Where's your sense of humor! Lucien?"

"You can have everything back," said Lucien. "You can have it all."

"You sound exactly like a man coming out of surgery," Emily laughed. She looked ravishing in this off-center attempt to appear cheap or to be in disguise, which was more likely what it was. "Besides that, I just can't figure where all this fits in. You've made so much of yourself."

The moon came straight down through the skylight, and the pool was empty except for Emily and Lucien, who swam in its depths. "I want it like poison," Emily said. "That's how I want it and that's how I'm going to get it." Her silvery hair was almost invisible floating out against the surface. She tilted her head back and looked straight through the skylight. "After that, I want you to give me a room right here at my old swimming hole."

The band was playing "Red River Valley." Lucien sat with the mayor and the rest of the party, nearly forty people including the convocation from their sister city. Flatware accumulated with course after course of Henchcliff's food. The little people were eating with their hands and radiating a rare and genial mood that affected the earnest citizens around them. Wick Tompkins was there too with the grin of a sprite. He tried their eating methods and praised them. Lucien called down the table to Wick, jumping his eyebrows in a gesture meant to break the ice. He said, "I have to talk to you." The little people stared around in incomprehension. Their elder, who spoke English, cried out, "Party time!" with a hopeful smile. Lucien went down to Wick's end of the table.

"Emily's here."

"I *thought* something was the matter with you."

"I don't know what to do."

"Have yourself a couple of belts. You've got a speech to make." Wick was wearing a striped suit, and his face was as blank as that of a bystander at an excavation. "I'm afraid you're all alone on this one."

"The trouble is, I still have some feeling for Emily."

"No, Lucien," said Wick. "You love Suzanne and little what's-his-name, little four-eyes."

"*Speech! Speech! Speech!*" They were clapping their hands and repeating the imprecation while looking straight at Lucien. He returned to his seat and stood for a moment until it was quiet. Then he spoke of his town and his country and his life. He was not afraid of losing his listeners. He knew he still had them as he talked about children and the next world. When he sat down they applauded while the elder and his closest aides cried out, "Top brands!" with such merriment and accord and humanity that in it was a kind of sacrament between them all. Lucien couldn't imagine where it was coming from.

When the meal was finished and the milling began, Lucien returned to the house and went upstairs. Emily was stretched out on the bed with her hands over her forehead like a cloth. He couldn't see her eyes. "I hope that you can appreciate that I am coming off an extremely checkered year."

"I understand," said Lucien, aching with sympathy.

"Did the sad tale of W. T. Austinberry make it this far north?"

"Yes, it did."

"A sad tale for all."

"Yes," said Lucien, shocked.

"I shot him with this." She held up the pistol. It was a polished, thin, flat thing. Lucien felt a fleeting, mad regret that he hadn't found a way of exchanging W.T. for Kelsey. Then he knew it was crazy. It was alarming to feel the desire to go on rescuing Emily.

She reclined on her side. He found himself staring. "And don't imagine you're the only one who wonders why I am back. I had a vivid, I'm telling you vivid, life among those special American people who cannot return to the country. It is a superb club composed of the most interesting people that our society produces. You ought to look into it. Membership usually requires doing something awful, but where is it written life is to be easy? We even had a couple of Nazis. Not that I approve. But they were gentlemanly in all respects, and more than anybody else in the group, they seemed to know how to dress fashionably in the tropics. You know? The rest of us were rolling up our sleeves and gleaming with perspiration. I can only imagine we must have seemed pathetic. But that life down there takes time to learn. As I speak of it, Lucien, I grow more and more nostalgic. Obviously W.T. didn't fit into any of that. Till my dying day, I will see W.T. wearing cowboy boots on those beautiful beaches. And believe you me, whoever said the ones in the big hats are the premature ejaculators had that one right."

"Why weren't you tried?" Lucien asked.

"Some very good American friends found me one of those countries you can spit across, and we went there in a sport-fishing boat. And *that* little country was just full of people who couldn't go back to *their* little countries. So I found myself in a society that was entirely less attractive than the one I had just left. But if it could have been proven that I killed W.T., it was because in his desperate, misguided adoration of me he began to behave just exactly as my husband had, though he never quite reached the heights of beating me, slamming my hands in car doors, selling my piano and all but kenneling me. In short, I have not had clear sailing. Do you think I have?" She was crying, her rage and grief showing all at once.

Lucien was tormented. He had to get out of there. He told Emily that he had to be at the spring by closing time and went out of the house, leaving her upstairs with the curtains blowing.

The bar was still nearly full of customers. When Lucien walked in, Wick cried out from a bar stool, " 'Lord, have mercy on my son, for he is a lunatic and sore vexed. For ofttimes he falleth into the fire and oft

169

into the water.'—Matthew seventeen."

"That's nice," said Lucien coldly. "Everyone should read the Bible. It's not getting the play in bars it once did."

"Are you gonna stand there till you fall to China?" said Wick drunkenly. "Or are you gonna drink?"

"Drink." Lucien sat at the bar.

"Lucien," said Wick, "there's a time to try and a time to fly and a smart bird knows why."

"How true," said Lucien with sarcastic tolerance. The bartender set their drinks down. Wick brought him into focus, then pushed some money his way.

"Excuse me," said Wick to the bartender, "but you're shitting in my wallet."

"Why don't you go home and go to bed," said Lucien. Wick gulped his drink and stood up haughtily.

"I wonder if you know who you're talking to," said Wick while everyone looked on. "I'm currently starring in the life story of an elderly auto dealer, now appearing at the Mark Taper Forum in Los Angeles, which features endless laughter from a fortune-teller's booth and other modern situations. History at its most informative. Do come back and see me in my dressing room. Free mints. Standing ashtrays. Others like yourself from the smart set. At the end of the play they pin a big paper daisy to my chest and hand me a piece of spoiled fish. The curtain falls to immense applause, mostly for me."

He took one step and passed out.

Lucien walked around past the spring. It was now quiet, and he tried to imagine it as it had been when he was here with his father and the cloud of crows lifted from its surface into the sky. He thought of the poem where death leaves a hole for the lead-colored soul to beat the fire. And he thought of the days he floated the river alone, carrying a life jacket in his son's size.

Lucien could tell from a distance that Suzanne's light was still on, the windblown shrubbery turning its glow into semaphore. Inside, Suzanne sat beside a table reading. She wore a sweater over her bathrobe. "Where have you been?" she asked.

"You knew I had that dinner."

"Yes—?"

"And Emily is here," said Lucien. Suzanne's eyes were so blank it was as if the optic nerve had died.

"*Is* she."

"I thought I had better tell you that."

"Why don't you not talk about it, Lucien." She turned her book onto its front.

"Okay."

"But when you see her, remember how well I've been doing on my own. And no matter what, it might be years before I trust you again. It might be never."

Lucien said, "I'll take that chance."

Emily slept naked on top of the covers with her purse next to her. She woke up when he came in but barely moved. The security light broke through the venetian blinds and striped everything. There was a light in the bathroom, too, and you could see half of the medicine cabinet and a wet washcloth hanging from the edge of the sink. Digital numbers glowed on the clock radio and it was very quiet. Lucien asked her to get dressed, and she stood up and started dressing; the stripes of light divided her body. Lucien watched.

"I'm in your hands, aren't I? Especially if I like where we're going. Because mystery is glamour and vice versa. That's what courtship is all about. People court love—

reach me those shoes—and they court death. All the big things are courted. Where are we going?"

"To get you a plane. I'm sending you away."

"What if I don't go?"

"I'm not sure. I guess the police will find you."

"You absolutely will not hide me?"

"That's right. I could sell the place and send you whatever it brings. I could do that."

"No, darling, you should keep it. It fits you like a glove. It would be like defacing a painting to separate you from your sideshow." He knew she still had the gun, and when she gazed at him, he felt her weigh him neatly. It was a privileged, eerie look at eternity.

They drove on until the starlight on the prairie showed the winding road like a piece of string. There were huge dry-land farms on either side of them where the wheat had been cut in panels of design and immensity. The cool night wind crossed the cropland and entered the sedan. Whatever it was that was happening to Lucien seemed as if it could have come from some source thousands of years or thousands of miles away.

"Do you understand that if you send me away it might be the end of me?"

"Yes, I do," he said, and he felt suddenly uprooted, a feeling as violent as childbirth. Light jumped at them from the airfield, and a clamor of wind from the croplands filled the interior of the car. Lucien stopped. He got a dime from her and called the pilot. A light went on in a trailer a few hundred yards away.

"Do you remember when you came home from your broken marriage and your shattered wifette and made that wonderfully infantile gesture of paying my bail?"

"Why do you call it infantile?"

"Because I could perfectly well have paid it myself."

"I thought it meant something when you let me do it."

"It did mean something! It meant that the ranch would not be seized when I left the country because it was in your name. It meant that I would always have it to come back to. That's how much contempt I had for you." The flashing light from the airfield ignited their faces.

"I'm sorry to hear that."

"I should think you would be. But you're not cruel, Lucien. That's what sets you apart from the others. On the other hand, you haven't faced much either."

"Are you going to kill me?"

"Don't flatter yourself."

Lucien stood out on the grass to watch the plane take off. It started across the runway and swung into the wind. It was away in the dark when it left the ground and began to climb at a steady angle. In a very little time, Lucien couldn't tell its lights from the stars.

Suzanne rented a car because she wanted to drive across Wyoming with James and let him see the Wind River Range and the Red Desert, where the bands of mustangs could be seen from the road. They would turn the car in when they got to Denver and fly home. She said she wanted James to know she was a western girl even if they spent all their time in the city. James hung around his father's neck and kissed him goodbye and said he would see him next time. When the boy was in the car, Suzanne said, "He isn't afraid of you anymore. That's the best thing that's happened. Weren't you always afraid of your father?" She got into the car.

"I guess I was," said Lucien, "but he's long gone now."

Lucien's son waved back to him, and Suzanne kept her eye on the road.

173

## About the Author

THOMAS MCGUANE was born in Michigan and educated at Michigan State University, the Yale School of Drama and Stanford. He now lives in Montana.